So he was ha...
charming.

Considering his ties to the person she didn't
want in her life, those were liabilities, not
assets.

However, when she drove to work the next
morning and found a familiar black Lexus
parked in the lot, she added persistent to his
list of character traits. Ordinarily it would
have been a point in his favor.

She pulled into the stall next to his, narrowly
missing his feet as he leaned nonchalantly
against the driver's door. Because the top was
down, she glared at him from her seat.

'What are you doing here?'

Evan's killer grin appeared far too cocky. 'I'm
waiting for our day to begin.'

'What are you talking about?'

'Joe Campbell sent me.'

The name buzzed in her head like a swarm of
bees. 'What?'

'I'm your new doctor.'

NURSES WHO DARE

The Wyman sisters—
**women who conquer their fears and emotions
and win the lives and loves they long for.**

In A NURSE'S FORGIVENESS Marta Wyman must
find it in her heart to forgive her grandfather for the act
that estranged him from her mother before Marta was
born. Dr Evan Gallagher is in New Hope to persuade
her to forgive and forget—especially as it becomes
clear that they can't be together until she does.

In A NURSE'S PATIENCE Amy loves her job as a
nurse-practitioner until Dr Ryan Gregory joins the
practice and questions her abilities. She asks to work
with another physician—patience not being her strong
point. But if she persists she'll earn Ryan's trust and
much, much more!

In A NURSE'S COURAGE Rachel Wyman must find
the courage to go back to the nursing profession she
loves after she is robbed of her confidence when she is
unable to help a dying friend. Physician Nicholas
Sheridan is the man to help her rebuild her life. If she
can find the courage she'll not only win his trust, but
his love.

**Look out for A NURSE'S PATIENCE later in 2001
and A NURSE'S COURAGE in 2002**

A NURSE'S FORGIVENESS

BY
JESSICA MATTHEWS

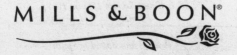

MILLS & BOON®

First published in Great Britain 2001
Harlequin Mills & Boon Limited,
Eton House, 18-24 Paradise Road, Richmond, Surrey TW9 1SR

© Jessica Matthews 2001

ISBN 0 263 82662 7

Set in Times Roman 10½ on 12¼ pt.
03-0501-37403

Printed and bound in Spain
by Litografía Rosés, S.A., Barcelona

CHAPTER ONE

THE photographs didn't do her justice.

Standing in front of the receptionist's desk at the New Hope Clinic, Evan Gallagher mentally congratulated himself on his good luck. He'd taken a huge risk by not calling ahead and learning if she was on duty, but under the circumstances he couldn't. Doing so would have jeopardized everything he was trying to accomplish by his unannounced visit.

In any case, the woman he'd come to see had just appeared in the doorway with a folder in hand and a stethoscope around her neck. So far, so good.

Now, if he could only talk to her before she realized just exactly who he was...

"Mrs Rochoa?" Marta Wyman asked, giving Evan a brief nod and a pleasant smile which he returned before she glanced past his shoulder.

The only other person in the waiting room, a stout lady in her mid-fifties, struggled to her feet, then slowly shuffled forward.

Evan noticed how the smile on Marta's face grew as she greeted her patient. He'd studied the eight-by-ten glossies in the private investigator's folder and had memorized Marta's features to the point he could easily have picked her out of a crowd.

Her high cheekbones, hazel eyes and auburn hair didn't come as any surprise to him, but the photos

5

hadn't captured the sensual slant to her mouth, the sparkle in her eyes, the proud tilt to her head, or the compassion in her heart as she grabbed Mrs Rochoa's arm to steady her balance.

Her concern for the woman seemed genuine, he noted critically. Then again, the investigator's thorough report had indicated she was well liked in this town of two thousand. Obviously her kindness extended to everyone...except the man Evan represented.

''Are you a little stiff today?'' Marta asked the lady. She'd restrained her hair in a tight knot at the back of her head, although a few loose tendrils framed her face. Idly, he wondered how long her hair would be if she let it hang freely.

Now that he stood within arm's reach, it struck him how those photos also hadn't prepared him for her trim form or the warmth in her husky voice. Her tone was completely different from the one he'd heard during their last, far-too-brief conversation. Now it reminded him of long evenings in front of a crackling fire, followed by even longer nights and breakfast in bed.

Clearly, the men of New Hope didn't recognize the jewel in their midst. According to his information, Marta Wyman had dated several men during her twenty-eight years, but those relationships had been more platonic than romantic in nature. Working on her education to become a nurse-practitioner while supporting her two younger stepsisters had occupied most, if not all, of her time.

However, none of this explained why Marta refused to talk to anyone even remotely connected to the man who was her only surviving blood relative.

As a result, Evan had decided to conduct his mission in person. Marta wouldn't be able to leave him talking to dead air on the telephone like the last time. Neither could she throw him out on his ear. She might have taken a self-defense class, which was a good idea considering some of the unsavory characters he'd seen on a few street corners, but he'd learned a few tricks of his own during his childhood in rough surroundings. And at six-two, he had an eight- or nine-inch advantage over her.

"My joints are all stoved up," Mrs Rochoa answered ruefully. "It's this humid weather we're having."

"I understand. You're not the only one suffering," Marta commented.

Watching the older woman's stiff gait and the solicitous way Marta ushered her through the door, Evan pegged her as a lady plagued with arthritis. He sympathized. He knew what it was like for one's wishes to war with one's body. His recent viral infection had taught him that particular lesson. Surely by the end of his vacation he'd be fighting fit once again.

As soon as the two disappeared behind the door, Evan faced the blonde receptionist in her mid-twenties, idly noting her wheelchair while she chatted on the phone. Her name tag read "Rosalyn", and he forced himself not to tap the bell on the counter. His sole reason for being here was to meet Marta, and antagonizing the guardian of her time wasn't a wise move to make.

As if she'd read his thoughts, Rosalyn said a cheery goodbye into the receiver before she finally acknowledged his presence.

"May I help you?" she asked.

He flashed her a huge smile. "I'd like to see—"

Rosalyn tapped the battered clipboard on the ledge in front of him with a short red fingernail. "Sign in."

Evan glanced around the waiting room. "But I'm the only one here."

"*Everyone* signs in," she said, her smile offsetting her firm tone. "No exceptions."

Fine. He could play by the rules. Evan scrawled his name, using the cheap ink pen someone had affixed to the board via a long piece of string. With any luck, Rosalyn wouldn't recognize his name.

"I only need a few minutes…"

She arched one light brown eyebrow. "Have you been here before?"

"No."

"First visits take thirty minutes, give or take a few."

"I'm glad to hear she's thorough." Thirty uninterrupted minutes with Marta. Surely his powers of persuasion could do the job in that length of time.

"If you're a drug rep or a salesman you should have come before nine. You'll have to wait until tomorrow."

Evan had purposely worn casual clothes to avoid notice and speculation. He'd visited enough small-town Americana to know that a man wearing a suit was either headed to a funeral or not to be trusted. He flashed her another smile, guaranteed to soften the most hard-hearted.

"I'm not a salesman. I just want to speak to—"

Before he could finish his statement, Marta appeared behind Rosalyn. At the same time Mrs Rochoa walked through the waiting-room door.

Rosalyn ignored him to wave at the Hispanic woman. "See you next month," she called out.

"If not before," Mrs Rochoa answered as she headed for the exit.

Evan cleared his throat. "I thought I could see—"

Once again, he was interrupted. This time Marta was responsible as she addressed Rosalyn in a low tone.

"Any news from our *friend*?" Her emphasis on the last word suggested the person in question was anything but.

Rosalyn shook her head. "Sorry."

"I swear I'm going to choke that man when he finally shows up," she ground out, wearing an expression as dark as the sky during a summer storm. "He knows better than to pull this stunt again. And if he doesn't, he certainly should! Talk about a useless waste of skin…"

Her fiery indignation almost made Evan glad for the partition separating him from the two women. Even so, he noticed how Marta didn't pay him a second glance as she vented her anger. He didn't feel guilty for eavesdropping. After all, he'd been there first.

Rosalyn turned her back to Evan as she answered her boss. "Don't you mean *if* he shows up?"

Marta tossed her head and waved aside the comment. "When. If. It doesn't matter. He's going to get a piece of my mind and so will his so-called boss. They'll either hear it in person or on the phone. I've had enough of this nonsense." She muttered something under her breath that Evan suspected was unflattering and probably unladylike.

"What shall I do? Try to locate him?"

Marta's shoulders visibly slumped and her mouth formed a tight line as she considered the request. "We've paged him before and he hasn't answered. We'll give him until one-thirty. If he isn't in the building by then, I'm taking matters into my own hands. I'll camp on his doorstep, if I have to."

Turning on one heel, she stomped out of Rosalyn's office.

Considering the shabby appearance of New Hope's clinic, Evan pictured the nameless "he" as a repairman who had placed Marta's request on the bottom of his priority list.

Rosalyn turned around to reach for the phone, then froze as soon as she saw Evan.

Once again, he smiled at her. "I'd like to see Marta."

"Is this an emergency?"

Evan wasn't accustomed to anyone questioning his actions. Although he was one of the younger members of the internal medicine department at St Margaret's Hospital in Dallas, he was also the one who singlehandedly raked in more donations for their facility than any other physician. Respect simply came with the territory.

An urge to raise an eyebrow in a manner capable of cutting lofty interns and medical students down to size came over him, but he stifled the impulse. If he hadn't wanted to maintain a low profile and slip past Marta's defense systems, he shouldn't have dressed the part.

At the same time, he admired Rosalyn for guarding Marta Wyman's time so closely. His own secretary could take a few lessons from her.

He cleared his throat. "No, but it's rather urgent."

"Are you ill?"

Evan considered his answer, wondering if she'd noticed his pallor. After contracting hepatitis A from contaminated shellfish at a dinner party, he'd decided to turn his convalescence into an extended vacation. He was past the contagious stage and easily could have resumed his patient load, but he simply wasn't physically or emotionally ready.

There was nothing like a bout of serious illness to encourage one to reassess priorities, which was why he was on his way to Breckenridge, Colorado for a few more weeks of peace and quiet. His stop in New Hope was only a detour in order to perform a favor for a man he admired.

"I've been ill. Yes." Evan didn't see the need to explain in detail. Perhaps the news would appeal to Rosalyn's sympathies and she would usher him into Marta's presence stat.

Rosalyn thrust another clipboard at him. "Fill out this questionnaire, please. All six pages. Since you don't have an appointment, she'll work you in, but you'll have a long wait.''

He glanced around the waiting room. ''Why? No one's here.''

''We're officially closed until one-thirty for lunch.''

Perhaps if he piqued Rosalyn's interest… ''I'm not here for Marta's medical expertise.''

A puzzled frown appeared on Rosalyn's face. ''I don't understand.''

He mentally crossed his fingers and hoped she wouldn't recognize his name. At least, not immediately.

''I'm Dr Evan—'' He stopped as soon as he saw Rosalyn's face blanch.

''Oh, my. We've been waiting for you.''

Now it was his turn to be surprised, but he recovered quickly. He'd only made his decision to contact Miss Wyman thirty-six hours ago and he hadn't breathed a word to anyone.

Rosalyn backed up her wheelchair and rolled out of her office. A moment later she reappeared in the same doorway Mrs Rochoa had recently passed through.

''You should have spoken up sooner,'' she chided as a distinctly pink hue colored her face. ''With this being your first time here, I didn't know who you were. I apologize for making you wait, Dr Evans.''

Dr Evans. They had been waiting for a *physician* and not a repairman. No wonder the lioness guarding the door had turned into a lamb. After the conversation he'd overheard, damage control was in order.

Under other circumstances, he would have done the honorable thing and corrected her false impression. However, desperate times called for desperate measures. If deceiving Rosalyn for a few minutes allowed him to carry out his personal agenda, then he could live with this white lie on his conscience.

"No problem," he said calmly, intent on carrying his charade as far as he could before Rosalyn deciphered his name from his scrawl on the clipboard. With any luck—and he believed one made one's own to a certain degree—she wouldn't notice the discrepancy until he and Marta reached an agreement.

Rosalyn expertly reversed and headed toward a small room at the end of the hallway, her wheels whispering against the tile floor. Evan followed, noting how the hallway seemed extra-wide, as if the old building had been remodeled with Rosalyn's disability in mind.

She rolled to a stop near the open door and waved him inside. "This is Marta's office. If you'll wait here, I'll send her in. She'll brief you on what needs to be done."

He couldn't help himself. "Should I have brought a bodyguard?"

Rosalyn's face turned a brighter shade of pink and she avoided his gaze. "Marta was just letting off steam. We've expected you for the past two Wednesdays. She's a firm believer in the philosophy of 'three strikes and you're out'."

He filed that piece of information away, certain it would come in useful. Success often depended on using those useful bits he'd stored in his head.

"And today would have been strike three," he commented.

"Yes."

Marta certainly wouldn't think kindly of him for impersonating the absent Dr Evans. Then again, Dr Evans clearly wasn't high on her list of favorite people anyway, so Evan didn't have anything to lose.

"Thanks for the warning," he said dryly.

Rosalyn shrugged. "Just thought you should know."

"I appreciate the tip."

"If you'll excuse me?" Without waiting for his dismissal, she rolled away, leaving him to marshal his thoughts.

Friends and colleagues claimed he had a silver tongue because of his astonishing success at coaxing the most reluctant of potential donors into digging deep in their pockets. What most people *didn't* know was that his success came about because he searched for the individual's weak spot, then played upon it.

He had a good idea of Marta's vulnerability and he intended to use his educated guess to his advantage. He owed Winston Clay a debt that couldn't be repaid and so, no matter how poor he thought Ms Wyman's behavior, he didn't intend to fail.

Between the private investigator's report and his earlier failed mediation attempt, he knew the situation with Ms Wyman required careful handling. Considering her attitude toward the hapless Dr Evans, her mood wouldn't improve once she learned the reason behind Evan's spur-of-the-moment visit.

He'd put his personal feelings of distaste for her

aside, tread lightly and appeal to her nurturing nature. If that didn't work, the prospect of money would. He hadn't met a woman yet whose eyes didn't light up when cash was mentioned. Once Marta heard what Winston could offer her and her stepsisters, she'd jump at the opportunity to include him in her small family circle.

He'd experienced enough of life to know when people were trying to up the ante. Winston was a proverbial goldmine and Marta had to know it. It wouldn't surprise Evan if she was simply being difficult in order to hold out for the most she could. If Evan had been in Winston's shoes, he would have dismissed her from his mind after she'd refused to speak to him. She would lose the most by being stubborn, not Winston.

However, he wasn't in Winston's position. The elderly man had put up a brave front in the face of Marta's rejection, but Evan had seen how his shoulders had become more stooped, his mouth more pinched, his eyes more dull with each passing day. His loss of spirit had pained Evan and he was determined to bring the spring back to Winston's step.

Then, and only then, would he begin to relax, enjoy his vacation and work out his own prescription for happiness.

Marta tugged Mrs Taylor's medical record from its slot in the wall-to-ceiling shelving unit. One way or another, Monica Taylor would be seen by a physician today even if she had to personally drive the woman to Joe Campbell's clinic. After all, the New Hope

Clinic was a satellite of Joe's practice in Liberal. As such, he was legally bound to oversee the care she gave the New Hope residents and make himself or one of his colleagues available for consultation. Maybe the illustrious Dr Campbell needed to be aware of his newest staff physician's failure to fulfill their end of their agreement.

On the other hand, maybe he knew and didn't care.

She squared her shoulders. New Hope might be small and off the beaten track, but its people deserved proper medical care just like those in the city. She wouldn't let Campbell get by with only tossing her the crumbs of his staff doctors' time.

If not for the fellow in her lobby, she'd be tempted to jump in her car, pick up Monica at her home and head to Liberal. And while she was there, she could easily search out another medical practice with physicians who would be committed to oversee her small outreach clinic.

The mere thought of the man waiting to see her conjured up his sharp, focused, mental image.

Thank goodness Mrs Rochoa had required her full attention, otherwise she could easily have stood in the doorway and melted under the impact of his killer smile. The curve of his mouth and the twinkle in his coal-black eyes had changed his nice-looking face into one she thought devastatingly handsome. He was a charmer, all right, packaged in the most delectable body a woman could ask for.

He was tall and lean and held himself with an easy grace. His short hair was the color of dark chocolate and appeared as soft and as touchable as a baby's.

His pleasant but youthful features had maturity written on them and a few crinkled lines radiated from his eyes. Early to mid-thirties, Marta decided.

The question was, why had he stopped to see her? She knew most of the townspeople and had never seen him before in her life. He was too striking an individual for her to have forgotten even a brief introduction. As far as the gossip went, no one was moving to their fair community, so he couldn't be a new resident. Most likely, he was simply passing through town.

A salesman. The idea flitted into her mind and instantly seemed to fit him like a surgical glove. Even without the suit and tie, he seemed too self-confident, too suave, and much too sexy to be anything else. As one of her patients liked to tell her, 'If it looks like a duck and acts like a duck, then it *is* a duck.'

Thanks to the absent Dr Evans, however, she wasn't in the mood for a long-winded sales pitch.

The door to their records storage room flung open and Rosalyn wheeled herself inside. ''Are we in for it now,'' she whispered, her blue eyes wide with panic.

''Now what?''

''You know that cute guy who's been in the waiting room all this time?''

''Yeah, so?''

''He's the doctor we've been waiting for,'' Rosalyn hissed.

The idea was too inconceivable to be believed. ''The salesman?''

Rosalyn drew her eyebrows together. ''Salesman?''

"Never mind. Anyway, it's a little late for jokes. April Fools' Day was two months ago."

"It's true," Rosalyn insisted. "He's Dr Evans."

A knot formed in the pit of Marta's stomach and her breakfast bowl of Cheerios threatened to stage a repeat appearance. "You're kidding."

"I wish I was," Rosalyn mourned. "But he's being really nice about the whole thing."

"What do you mean by 'the whole thing'?"

"I apologized for the wait and for your, um, little outburst."

Marta wished for the floor to open and swallow her. Heat spread up her neck. "You didn't."

"I did," her colleague said. "After all, he heard you going on and on so I had to say something to defend you. Anyway, he didn't act upset. Actually…" She tapped an index finger to her mouth. "Amused was more like it."

This day was going from bad to worse. "Amused? Well, let's hope he stays that way. Where is he?"

"In your office."

Marta drew a bracing breath and rubbed at the ache under her breastbone—the same ache that had become an almost constant companion after the private investigator had invaded her quiet existence several weeks ago. "OK. Pull everyone's chart who was scheduled to see the doctor this morning. And call them to start coming at one-thirty. It'll make for a long day, but I'm not letting him leave until he's seen every last person."

"Will do." Rosalyn studied Marta for a long moment. "Are you all right?"

She managed a smile. "Yeah. A few antacids and I'll be fine."

Rosalyn raised one eyebrow. "If you say so."

"I do. Now, go on so I can formally meet our Dr Evans."

"Just remember you can catch more flies with honey than vinegar."

Marta raised one eyebrow. "I don't want or need another fly in my life. In Dr Evans's case, he's more 'fly in the ointment' than anything."

"Humph."

"Don't worry. I'll be polite. I can't afford to run him off now that he's finally found time for us."

In spite of Marta's attempt to sound confident, the butterflies inside her stomach suggested the opposite. She shouldn't have grumbled about him in such a public place where even the walls had ears. Luckily, she hadn't blurted out his name or said anything truly defamatory. Maybe she could bluff her way through this.

Then again, Rosalyn had already apologized, so bluffing was out. She crossed her fingers in the hopes that Rosalyn was correct—that Dr Evans hadn't taken offense at her unflattering remarks. Already, she was cringing over her waste-of-skin comment when his skin covered the finest example of a male she'd ever seen.

If luck was truly with her today, Ros had correctly read his reaction as amused rather than angry. Even so, she didn't intend to grovel. As far as she was concerned, he should be asking *her* forgiveness for leaving her in the lurch two weeks in a row.

A few steps from her office, she paused to square her shoulders. Clutching Monica Taylor's folder to her chest and pasting a smile on her face, she stopped on the threshold.

"Dr Evans. It's a pleasure to finally meet you."

The grin on his face suggested that he knew she was lying through her teeth. No doubt he'd heard her subtle emphasis on 'finally'.

"I'm glad to be here, myself," he began.

"We sent home your scheduled patients. I didn't see any point in making them wait when we weren't sure if you were coming or not. Ros is calling them back right now."

"Before she does, we need to talk."

"Don't worry. I'll brief you before you see them. There's nothing pressing, other than a few procedures I can't do—a few skin biopsies, for instance. The only serious case is Monica Taylor and I have her chart right here."

She held it out and was surprised to watch him stare at the folder as if it were a vial of anthrax.

"I have a confession to make," he said, meeting her gaze. "I'm not who you think I am."

His dark eyes were mesmerizing and it took Marta a few seconds to register what he'd said. "What?"

"I'm not Dr Evans. I'm Dr Evan Gallagher."

Marta blinked as she tried to make sense of it all and couldn't. "Dr Campbell didn't send you?"

His gaze grew even more intent as he shook his head. "I'm Dr Evan Gallagher."

Evan Gallagher.

Suddenly she understood why he'd paused and

hadn't offered any further explanation. He knew she'd recognize the significance of his name. She had, as soon as she'd stopped thinking in terms of Dr Evans.

Civility had immediately ceased being an option. Her temples pounded with a combination of anger and frustration at the audacity of this man. She'd stated her position plainly on the phone several weeks ago. She'd also expected him to call again, but he hadn't and so she'd thought the subject had died for lack of interest. She'd obviously been mistaken.

"You're good, you know that."

A puzzled wrinkle appeared on his forehead and his sharp eyes became wary. "How so?"

"Letting the weeks go by, so I'd feel as if I'd finally written 'the end' to that chapter of my life. You were only biding your time, waiting for me to let down my guard. Weren't you?"

He shook his head. "No. Winston respected your earlier decision. My visit today is strictly spur of the moment."

"If your explanation is supposed to appease me, it's not working."

She dropped the folder on the counter and turned toward the door. "I have nothing further to say to you, Dr Gallagher. Except goodbye."

With two quick steps, he blocked the exit. "All I'm asking you to do is listen."

"Listen? Why? There's nothing you can say that would possibly interest me."

"How will you know unless you hear me out?"

"I may not be a genius, *Dr* Gallagher, but your

very presence makes it easy for me to guess. You can drive back to Dallas and tell the man who claims to be my grandfather that my answer hasn't changed since the last time he asked you to call. It's still no.''

CHAPTER TWO

EVAN dropped his arm but continued to block the door with his body. "Winston didn't send me," he said. "He doesn't know I'm here."

Marta crossed her arms, narrowed her eyes and tapped one small foot on the tile floor. "And I suppose you just decided to go for a drive today and ended up several hundred miles from home. At least, I presume you also live in Dallas."

"More or less. Irving, to be more precise. As for going on a drive, I'm on my way to Colorado for some R and R."

"Then I won't keep you."

He held his ground, unwilling to lose this opportunity. "I'm not in any hurry."

"I am," she snapped. "Would you, please, move aside? I have patients who are coming to see a doctor who isn't here."

Evan had expected resistance. He would have been surprised if he hadn't encountered any.

"At least hear me out," he insisted. "Five minutes."

"I know what you're going to say. Winston Clay, the man who claims to be my grandfather, has finally discovered my whereabouts. Now he wants a reunion, so we can make up for lost time." She paused. "Am I right so far?"

He couldn't disagree. ''More or less.''

''For the record, I'm not interested. My mother's father disowned her twenty-eight years ago when she was unmarried and pregnant. If he wanted to appease his conscience, he should have made the effort while she was still alive.''

''He couldn't.''

''Why not?'' Marta raised an eyebrow. ''His millions weren't enough to make one long-distance phone call?''

''She disappeared,'' he said quietly.

She scoffed. ''How does an eighteen-year-old girl disappear from someone who has more resources at his disposal than the heads of some countries?''

Evan shrugged. ''There are ways. In any case, about a year after she left home he received word of her death and that of her child.''

''How is that possible? She didn't die until I was twelve. As far as I know, I still have a pulse.''

''I don't know how it happened,'' Evan said. ''But two months ago your grandfather received an anonymous tip concerning a grandchild. He hired a team of investigators and, in the process, they found you.''

Evan hadn't seen such excitement in Winston's eyes until the day the older man had had positive proof of a granddaughter in his hands.

''Isn't it funny how his high-priced *team* couldn't find us when the trail was fresh?''

''Apparently your mother had help in hiding her tracks. She changed her name and social security number before she married your stepfather. Once

Winston learned those facts, he didn't have any trouble locating you.''

Marta sauntered to her desk and sank into the chair. A furrow appeared across her forehead and she chewed on her lower lip before she swiveled to stare out the window. Clearly, this information was unexpected and she needed time to assimilate it. At least she was listening.

Part of Evan's success hinged on his ability to read people. Right now, she was wavering; he sensed it. His confidence grew and he moved closer.

''He'd like to talk,'' he said to the back of her chair.

For a long moment, she didn't answer. Evan, however, was patient. He didn't intend to leave until he'd wheedled an agreement out of her. As the minutes ticked by, he could almost taste victory. How could she refuse?

He pressed on. ''Wouldn't you like to meet him? Satisfy your curiosity?''

She continued to stare out the window and when she spoke her voice sounded…different, emotionless. ''I'm not curious about Winston Clay. I know all I care to know about him.''

''How can you say that?''

''New Hope may not be a bustling metropolis, but we're beyond the days of the pony express. We get newspapers and magazines on a daily basis.''

He shook his head. ''Reading an article isn't the same thing as meeting someone, talking to them.''

She spun around. ''I have. Met him, that is.''

He was stupefied. ''Where?''

"In his office. We spoke briefly. For about two minutes."

He wondered why Winston had never mentioned her visit. "When?" he pressed.

"Does it matter?"

Marta's calm voice frustrated him. "Of course it matters!"

"I disagree. As far as I'm concerned, the incident belongs in the past and that's where I intend to keep it. He has his life and I have mine."

Evan couldn't believe the older man would have spared only a few minutes to catch up with his long-lost granddaughter, no matter how busy his schedule. Unless...

"I'm sure he didn't know who you were," he began.

"He knew. He just didn't care to believe me or hear my story."

The reason behind her stubborn refusal to co-operate became clear. Evan had categorized her as cold and unfeeling when, in fact, her apparent apathy masked a painful combination of hurt and anger. Her attitude was simply part of her defense system.

The situation was more complicated than he'd thought. He needed more than persuasion...he needed a bulldozer to tear down the concrete wall she'd built to separate herself from her grandfather...

Evan leaned over and planted both palms face down on the desk. "When did you meet him? How old were you?"

She stood. "I refuse to be interrogated in my own

office. Your five minutes are up and this subject is closed.''

''Whatever happened back then,'' Evan said as he straightened, ever the peacemaker although he intended to discover exactly what *had* occurred and when, ''your grandfather wants to make amends for the choices he made. He's not a young man any more.''

''None of us are getting younger,'' Marta reminded him, holding his gaze. ''Since you're a physician, I suppose you're going to tell me he's dying of some incurable illness and wants to put his affairs in order before he meets his Maker.''

He'd considered using that angle, but had discarded the idea as being too melodramatic. ''If I did, would it convince you to at least speak with him on the phone?''

She pursed her lips and her eyes sent enough sparks in his direction to start a grass fire after a heavy rain. Most women in his social sphere had learned how to play cat-and-mouse games at their mothers' knees. It was a surprising change to deal with one whose face so clearly reflected her feelings. So far, he'd seen everything from cool disdain to outrage.

An unexpected desire to experience her passion flooded over him, along with a wave of jealousy toward the man who would kindle those fires.

Evan stopped short. Dammit, what was he thinking? He liked women who were sophisticated, eventempered and smelled of a designer fragrance. Marta was down-to-earth, had the disposition of a cactus and smelled of herself and rubbing alcohol. And yet she seemed sexier than anyone he'd ever dated.

He needed his vacation worse than he'd thought. He truly had lost his perspective if someone so close-minded and aggravating, someone who carried enough baggage to fill an airplane, turned him on.

"No."

Evan rubbed the back of his neck and managed a smile. "I didn't think so. Your grandfather is the picture of health for a seventy-five-year-old."

"I'm not surprised. Money can certainly make life easier in more ways than one."

He jumped at the opportunity she'd given him. He'd never known a woman whose attitude didn't change when cold, hard currency entered the picture, especially one who'd lived a hand-to-mouth existence as she had.

"Your grandfather is a wealthy man," he agreed. "He'd be extremely generous to you and your family."

If Marta's gaze could have ignited wet tinder before, the rays shooting out of her eyes would have melted him instantly. The sunlight streaming through the window made her hair shimmer as if it had been kissed by flames.

"And you think his financial *generosity* will make a difference to me." She spoke softly, but her clenched fists and squared shoulders contradicted her pleasant tone.

"To some, it might," he answered carefully, gauging her response. He'd expected to see a speculative gleam at his suggestion, not righteous indignation. Once again, he had to revise his opinion of her.

"I don't know who you are or how you figure into this equation, but I'm not one of those shallow socialites you're apparently used to associating with. My grandfather could own a dollar-bill-growing tree, and it wouldn't make a difference to me.

"Furthermore," she continued, without taking a breath, "if he wants to appease his conscience, he can donate to a worthy cause instead. I've lived without his assistance for the past twenty-eight years. I can manage the rest of my life without it, too."

Marta's vehemence clearly wasn't an act in order to sweeten the pot. She meant every word. Evan, however, refused to admit defeat so early in the game. "But—"

"But nothing. I'll give you an A for effort, Dr Gallagher, but my decision stands. 'No' is my final answer. You can continue on your vacation with a clear conscience.

"If you'll excuse me, I have to locate a missing doctor." She strode toward the door and flung it open. Stepping aside, she waved him through. "Have a nice trip to Colorado."

Evan let out a frustrated sigh. He'd clearly reached an impasse and further arguing wouldn't advance his cause.

"Thank you for your time," he said politely before he walked from the room.

The look of stunned surprise on Rosalyn's face as he headed for the exit was near comical, but he wasn't in the mood to be entertained. He acknowledged the receptionist with a nod and strode into the sunshine, well aware that the explanations would fall to Marta.

His mind raced to consider his next move, but he was short on brilliant ideas. The situation was far more complex than he'd thought. This wasn't a matter of reuniting two people who would then live happily ever after. Their past meeting, if one could truly call it such, had obviously been so upsetting that Marta had responded by rejecting anything to do with her grandfather.

Evan might have misjudged her motives, but after today's conversation he knew the value she placed on her principles. He wouldn't make the same mistake twice.

On the other hand, he wondered if Marta had realized her verbal slip when she'd referred to Winston as her grandfather. Those two words weren't much, but she had used them and so he chose to look on her recognition as a hopeful sign.

Marta might think the subject was closed, but it was far from over. As eager as he was for his month of solitude with only wildlife for company, he knew he wouldn't find the peace he'd been searching for until he'd resolved this situation to his satisfaction. Winston was like his own grandfather, and he didn't want to see him suffer any more than he already had.

Whatever Marta's problem, she would simply have to face it…and get over it.

To reach that point, however, he had to implement a back-up plan, which he didn't have at the moment. A familiar tug of weariness seemed to grow stronger—the beginnings of the bone-deep exhaustion that he hated and couldn't seem to shake.

Sliding behind the wheel of his Lexus, he suddenly realized Marta's true weakness and how he could use it to his advantage. All he needed was a phone number…

"Want to tell me what went on down the hall?" Rosalyn sat behind her desk, her arms folded across her chest as she stared up at Marta.

"He wasn't Dr Evans," Marta said shortly, watching Evan slide stiffly into his car—a shiny black Lexus that appeared out of place in the weed-infested, pothole-filled parking lot. "He's Dr Gallagher."

Rosalyn's eyes seemed to double in diameter. "The guy who's a friend of your grandfather?"

"Yes."

She snatched the clipboard off the counter and examined the sign-in sheet. "I should have looked at the name before you sent him in."

"I'll say."

"Still," Rosalyn continued on a reverent sigh, "I wish my grandad had friends like that."

"Hah! Just remember. Birds of a feather flock together."

"And your point is?"

"Winston Clay is a business tycoon. He didn't make it where he is today by being sweet, kind or generous. Underneath that polished veneer, he makes and breaks people with the stroke of his pen, without giving them a second thought."

"And how do you know his character so well?"

Rosalyn studied her carefully. "You're not keeping tabs on him, are you?"

"Don't be ridiculous," Marta snapped. "What Mr Clay does with his life doesn't concern me."

"Yeah, right."

"For your information, he's graced the cover of all the major magazines at one time or another, not to mention making the financial news headlines on a regular basis. A person would have to be living under a rock in the Pacific to not have heard about him."

"Golly. Dr Gallagher is just as famous?"

Marta gritted her teeth. "Who knows? The truth is, if my grandfather considers Dr Gallagher his friend, and vice versa, then the two of them are alike. Two peas in the same pod, so to speak."

Rosalyn shrugged. "You may be right, but Dr Gallagher is a twelve on a handsome scale of one to ten and you can't deny it."

Marta let out a sigh. Mother Nature had played a horrible and unfair trick by gifting her grandfather's lackey with exceptional, heart-stopping good looks. Claiming otherwise, though, wouldn't change reality.

"He may be nice-looking, but don't let his pretty face fool you, Ros," she warned. "He's like the tin man from the *Wizard of Oz*."

Rosalyn shook her head. "I disagree. He's got a heart all right. It beats pure male."

"Would you please take your mind off his body? I'm sure he's already filled the pages in his second little black book."

"Too bad my name isn't in it," the receptionist said, dreamy-eyed. "Seriously, though, he must want to get you and your grandfather together. Otherwise why would he have come to New Hope?''

Through the window in Ros's office, Marta had a perfect view of Dr Gallagher's car in the parking lot. To her surprise, the Lexus hadn't moved an inch. Even from this distance, she could see him holding a cellphone to his ear.

Checking in with Winston, she supposed wryly.

''He said he'd been ill,'' Ros supplied helpfully.

Which explained why he was on his way to Colorado for a vacation, but didn't say much for why he'd stopped in New Hope to plead Winston's case for the second time in four weeks.

No, Evan Gallagher had an ulterior motive and somehow Winston was involved. Marta would bet her new stethoscope on it. ''You may choose to give him altruistic motives, but I'm not that gullible,'' she said. ''In any case, it doesn't matter because he's leaving.''

She watched the Lexus reverse before it slowly crawled forward to the intersecting street. Even at the slow pace, the tires kicked up a haze of dust thick enough to obscure his Texas license plates. She should have been thrilled over her victory in this particular battle of wills, because this time she'd locked the door to a painful part of her past.

If not thrilled, she should at least feel some satisfaction. After all, she'd made her wishes clear. Dr Gallagher, or anyone else for that matter, now knew not to waste his time trying to reopen the subject.

This was for the best, she reassured herself. Her stepsisters and her patients filled her life to the brim.

More specifically, she didn't have the time or the desire to play Winston Clay's games.

And Winston Clay was a master at playing games. On the few occasions when her mother had spoken of her forceful parent, Marta had heard of how easily her grandfather manipulated people to do his bidding.

Marta didn't intend to be another chess piece on his playing board.

"He'll be back," Ros predicted as she tapped the clipboard with her pen.

Marta tore her gaze away from the disappearing Lexus and glanced at her friend. "And what makes you say that?"

Ros shrugged. "The doctor doesn't seem the type to give up so easily."

"What else can he do? He stated his case and I gave him my final answer. Dr Gallagher is on his way to Colorado even as we speak."

Rosalyn slowly shook her head. "I wouldn't bet money on it."

"Oh, for heaven's sake. Dr Gallagher knows how I feel about Winston Clay. I doubt if he's willing to hang around New Hope on the off chance I might— notice, I said *might*—change my mind."

"I tell you, Marta, he'll be back," Ros insisted. "Look at the way he signed his name."

Marta glanced at the line the receptionist had indicated. "Yeah. So?"

"Someone who takes pride in his success often writes his name in large letters, just like he did. He's a man who doesn't like to fail. I'd bet my next paycheck on it."

"He may not like to fail, but he did," she said firmly. "I'm sure I convinced him to leave me alone."

Ros frowned as she cocked her head to study the page. "I'm not so sure."

"Analyzing handwriting may be your hobby, but aren't you reading more into this than you should?" Marta asked.

"This isn't a parlor game or hocus-pocus," Ros insisted. "I've pegged a lot of people correctly and you know it. Remember the guy who refused to pay his bill? I warned you weeks ahead of time about him."

"Lucky guess. Plus, you'd seen his name listed on the police record in the newspaper."

"That was after I'd already told you my suspicions. He wasn't the only one either. What about Maria McAlister? I could tell from the way she wrote her first name smaller than her surname that she wasn't happy in her marriage. Six months later, she and Andy divorced."

"They were both too young. The whole town knew it wouldn't last before they walked down the aisle."

Ros dismissed her with a wave of one hand. "Furthermore, I'm guessing Dr Gallagher has some personal problem on his mind."

"Like which road to take to Colorado?"

Ros rolled her eyes at Marta's caustic comment. "See how his Christian name is smaller and slants slightly more to the left than the rest of his signature? I'd say he has a conflict somewhere in his life." She sighed. "I can't imagine it being in his social life."

"I suppose you can tell that from his signature, too."

Ros grinned. "I figured it out from his fantastic body and his gorgeous face. His handwriting just confirms my opinion."

"Oh, really?"

"Don't be so skeptical."

"Sorry, but I can't help it."

"See the pressure of his writing?" Ros pointed to her example. "Compare his to the others. Strong, heavy strokes indicate sensuality. It was the first thing I noticed."

"Too bad you didn't recognize his name first. Our entire conversation could have been avoided."

Ros shrugged. "Sorry. I can't be Miss Perfect all the time. Mark my words, we haven't seen the last of the delectable Dr Gallagher."

"I hate to put a damper on your analysis of his character or his personal conflict, but we'll never know if you're right or not. The only issue I'm concerned with at the moment involves the *real* Dr Evans. Where do you suppose he is?"

"Maybe he's been in a car accident."

Marta shook her head. "Considering his track record for the past few weeks, a wreck doesn't rank high on my list of possibilities."

Ros reached for the phone. "I'll call and see what I can find out."

"On second thoughts," Marta mused as she perched on the edge of her receptionist's desk, "*I'll* call. This time, I'm not listening to any of Dr Evans's excuses."

"And what are you going to do?"

"I'm going over his head to his boss, Dr Campbell. Maybe if I threaten to bring a busload of my patients to their clinic *en masse*, he'll make a few changes."

"I'll keep my fingers and toes crossed." Ros peered past her to glance at the main entrance. "In fact, I think you could use some of that luck right now."

"Oh?"

"Don't look now, but Monica Taylor just drove by."

Marta turned to glance out the window and saw the battered four-door sedan pull into a parking stall. She sighed as she rose.

Not only was Monica difficult to get along with at times, but she always seemed to present with the same complaints. Chest pain, aches and pains, or severe gastrointestinal upset.

More often than not, Marta couldn't find a cause for her problems. She'd instruct her patient to purchase appropriate over-the-counter medications which seemed to take care of the problem because Monica never returned with the same symptoms two weeks in a row. Each time the woman walked into the clinic Marta was reminded of how much she *didn't* know about the human body. Although Marta wanted a physician's opinion in case there was an underlying disease she had missed, Monica refused to make the thirty-mile trip.

Which was why Marta desperately wanted a physician in New Hope's clinic to evaluate her.

"I told Monica to come back today because the

doctor would be here," Marta said. "Now we'll have to send her home."

"Didn't we make an appointment for her to see Dr Campbell?" Ros asked.

"We've made several. She won't go."

"Why not?"

Marta shrugged. "She always has an excuse. It's either too far to drive or it will cost too much. I've tried to tell her that her health is worth more than anything, but she won't listen."

"She's an eccentric bird," Ros mentioned. "Rumor says she has more money stashed away than you or I will ever see in our lifetimes. Between her inheritances, good investments and her husband's life insurance settlement, her pockets are supposedly well lined."

"She certainly doesn't live like she's financially set for life." In her early sixties, Monica Taylor was a tall woman who suffered from a combination of poor fashion sense and apparent color-blindness. Shopping at garage sales and thrift stores was her favorite hobby and she wore her bargains without considering how well they complemented each other. Today, she modeled a pair of purple capri pants and a red-and-orange Hawaiian-print shirt.

"Yeah, well, what can I say? Believe me, she could easily afford to pay for a private staff of physicians." Ros refrained from further comment as the glass door swung open.

"Good afternoon, Mrs Taylor," she told her cheerfully.

"Hello, Rosalyn. Marta." Monica's mouth turned

into a tired but genuine smile. "I came to see the doctor, just like you told me."

"I'm sorry, but he hasn't arrived," Marta explained.

"Then I'll wait."

"We're not exactly sure when he's coming." Marta hated to say the words and vowed to give Dr Evans a good tongue-lashing at the next opportunity.

"How irresponsible of him," she declared. "I was hoping to finally see someone who could give me some answers."

Although Marta wanted that as well, hearing Monica emphasize "finally" cut her to the quick. It wasn't as if she hadn't done everything possible to help the woman. She bent over backwards fitting the woman into her schedule, regardless of how busy it was.

"I haven't been feeling too well these past few days," Monica continued. "My chest hurts."

"Why don't I listen and see what I can find?" Marta managed to swallow her aggravation enough to sound polite.

A few minutes later, in the nearest exam room, Marta took Monica's vitals before listening to her heart and lungs.

"Your lungs are clear," she said as she slung the stethoscope around her neck. "Your heart sounds as normal as it can be, but I'll run an ECG just to be on the safe side."

Monica acquiesced without a murmur. In no time at all Marta had affixed the leads and the heart tracing was traveling over the phone lines to Dr Campbell's clinic.

As soon as it was over, she helped the woman re-arrange her clothing and sit up. ''We'll have the re-port back from the doctor before long, if you'd like to wait.''

''All right. It's cooler here than in my apartment. A fan just doesn't do much in this heat.''

''The power company has a special program for low-income people. I'm sure if you talked to them, you could afford to cool your home.''

''Really? I'll have to check into that.''

Her lack of interest suggested just the opposite, but Marta couldn't make those arrangements for her. ''I'll be back as soon as I have the doctor's diagnosis.''

She used the phone in her office and dialed a num-ber from memory. ''This is Marta,'' she told Connie, Dr Campbell's receptionist. ''Dr Evans hasn't arrived at our clinic yet, and I wanted to find out how soon we could expect him.''

Connie's voice sounded tentative to the point of nervousness. ''I'll connect you with Dr Campbell. He can answer your questions.''

I certainly hope so. ''Thanks,'' Marta replied.

In what seemed like an instant, Joe Campbell's bar-itone carried over the phone line. ''Marta, we have a problem.''

''No joke. What I want to know is, is Dr Evans going to show up? Or, better yet, does he even exist?''

''He exists, but he hasn't worked out. His wife hated this part of the country and flew back to Kansas City within days of moving here. He tendered his two-week notice last week and I haven't seen him since.''

''You could have called me. I've had patients scheduled for days.''

''I know. I fully intended to come myself, but I simply haven't been able to get away.''

''So what am I supposed to do? We established this satellite clinic as a service to the people of New Hope. If we're expecting them to drive all the way to Liberal for every sniffle—''

''I'm working on a solution,'' he interrupted. ''In fact, I'm in the process of hiring a locum tenens for the next few weeks. I may even have one who can start tomorrow, but I don't have the details completely worked out.''

''Good,'' she said. ''Have you looked at the ECG I just sent you?''

''As we speak. I don't see any abnormalities. Any history of heart disease?''

''None. Just chest pain right now.''

''It's a normal tracing. Have you drawn blood for labs?''

''Not yet.''

''Go ahead. Might as well be thorough.''

''OK. And you'll phone about the locum later today?''

''Before five,'' he promised.

Marta replaced the receiver and returned her attention to Monica. ''Your ECG is fine,'' she said, ''but I'm going to draw a blood sample to check your heart enzymes.''

''And then can I go?''

''Yes.'' Marta quickly drew two vials of blood and

taped a cotton ball over the site. "I'll have the results tomorrow, so I'll call you."

"I don't have a telephone."

In this day and age of Internet access, fax machines and cellphones, it seemed inconceivable not to have a basic telephone line. "All right. Check with us right before lunch. I should have your report by then."

"I will."

The rest of the afternoon sped by. At four-thirty, Ros stopped her in the hallway. "Connie called. The new doctor will be here bright and early tomorrow morning."

"Did she say who it was?" His identity didn't matter as long as he had 'MD' after his name, but it would have been nice to have been better informed.

"No, but according to her we're lucky to have him. His specialty is internal medicine and he supposedly graduated at the top of his class."

Marta grimaced. "Great."

"What's wrong now? You've got a doctor coming—a specialist no less. What more could you want?"

"Think about it. If this guy is as good as Joe claims, what's he doing as a locum when he could be making a fortune with a practice of his own?"

"Good point."

"He's probably got the personality of a slug."

"It's possible," Ros agreed. "But you know what the old-timers say."

"No, what?"

"Beggars can't be choosers."

Ros was right. There was little Marta could do about the situation except wait until she took the nameless doctor's measure tomorrow. She hoped he'd be easy to work with, someone with a pleasant bedside manner. Someone like…

Evan Gallagher. Where had that thought come from? she asked herself crossly. So he was handsome, polite and charming. Considering his ties to the person she didn't want in her life, those were liabilities, not assets.

However, when she drove to work the next morning and found a familiar black Lexus parked in the lot, she added persistent to his list of character traits. Ordinarily, it would have been a point in his favor. Right now, because his tenacity had made them opponents, she counted it as a strike against him.

She pulled her white Jeep Wrangler into the stall next to his, narrowly missing his feet as he leaned nonchalantly against the driver's door, his arms crossed. Because the top was down to allow for Mother Nature's method of air-conditioning, she glared at him from her seat.

"My answer is still no," she warned.

"I haven't asked a question."

"Then what are you doing here?"

Evan's killer grin appeared far too cocky. "I'm waiting for our day to begin."

"What *are* you talking about?"

"Joe Campbell sent me."

The name buzzed in her head like a swarm of bees. The situation had suddenly become too bizarre to be believed. "What?"

"I'm your new doctor."

CHAPTER THREE

MARTA slammed her car door. "Impossible. You can't be our new physician."

Evan remained leaning against his Lexus, his arms folded in a picture of ease. "I am."

"What strings did you pull?" she demanded, certain he'd used her grandfather's considerable influence in some way.

"None at all. You needed a doctor and I was available."

"Right," she scoffed. "A hotshot doctor from Dallas with nothing to do. How did you know about Joe?"

"You told me."

"I couldn't have…" Her voice faded into nothingness. She remembered mentioning Joe Campbell's name while Evan had been trying to introduce himself.

"All right, so I did," she admitted crossly. "But it doesn't explain why you're here and not in Colorado, enjoying the mountain air."

"As I said, you have a need and Joe has graciously consented to let me fill it."

She narrowed her eyes. "For how long?"

His dark-eyed gaze didn't waver. "For as long as it takes."

It sounded like a vow. "For as long as *what* takes?" She knew, but wanted him to spell it out.

"To change your mind about your grandfather."

"There isn't enough time in the world for that."

He shrugged. "I think there is."

"You're committed to this, aren't you?"

"Yes."

Her stomach twisted into a knot. "Having you here is absolutely ridiculous."

"I thought it was a great solution. So did Dr Campbell."

"He would," she grumbled. "Why would anyone give up a scenic vacation in the Rocky Mountains? All you'll see in New Hope is plenty of horizon and acres of tumbleweeds."

"I like open spaces. According to the newspapers, tumbleweeds are all the rage back east. In Singapore and London, too."

"You're missing the point. You're not supposed to be here at *all*."

"I'm where I want to be."

"Ah," she said as understanding dawned. "You're not just a friend of my grandfather's. You're on his payroll, aren't you?"

"Sorry to ruin your theory, but my income comes from other sources. As for your grandfather, our relationship goes back a lot of years."

If Evan Gallagher wasn't Winston's physician, then his family had clearly moved in the same circles as her grandfather. It was the only logical connection between the two men.

"As I said before," he added in a patient tone,

"Winston doesn't know I'm here. He thinks I'm in Breckenridge. Or at least on the way there."

Marta folded her arms. "You really don't expect me to believe that, do you?"

He shrugged. "Believe it or not. I've given you the truth. Better yet, call your grandfather and ask him yourself."

"I would, but that's exactly what you want me to do, isn't it?"

He grinned. "Maybe. Maybe not. You won't know until you call."

"Sorry," she said, shaking her head, "I'm not falling for your trick. You'll have to try again."

"Suit yourself. Out of curiosity, would you like to discuss this inside? We're starting to attract attention, but I don't mind if you don't…" He inclined his head toward the street.

An ancient but well-maintained Pontiac slowed to a crawl. The head of its driver, Beatrice Higgins, barely cleared the steering-wheel, but it was apparent that the blue-haired woman's attention rested squarely on them rather than the road.

Marta inwardly groaned. Bea had a talent for sticking her nose in other people's business and an uncanny knack for being in the right place at the wrong time.

"This isn't settled," she warned.

"I didn't think it was."

Evan's affability irritated her no end. Screaming in frustration seemed like a way to release her frustration, but she refused to give him the satisfaction of knowing how much his presence bothered her.

As she unlocked the door, she wondered what she could do or say to send Evan Gallagher on his way. She felt like a blade of grass caught up in a tornado, tossed about with no escape until nature calmed the storm.

She led the way to her office where she tossed her crocheted tote bag on top of her cluttered desk. After drawing a fortifying breath, she asked, "Why don't we start again?"

"Fine by me," he said cheerfully. "Mind if I sit while we hash things over?"

Marta nodded, wishing she could crawl into bed and turn the clock back a few hours. While he sank into the padded chair opposite her desk, she pondered her situation.

Cool disdain hadn't worked. Neither had anger. He'd endured her outright rudeness with remarkable aplomb, too. Perhaps it was time to take another tack. Maybe if she explained her side of the story, he'd accept her decision and leave her alone.

Yes, that was her answer. She'd report the bare bones of the day when she'd gathered her courage and swallowed her pride because Rachel had convinced her to give Winston a chance to redeem himself. Just thinking about how he'd cold-heartedly trampled her self-esteem in just a few short minutes sent a stabbing pain through her chest and a fresh surge of acid into her stomach.

She rummaged in her desk and popped an antacid in her mouth, aware of Evan's gaze following her every move.

"Let me see if I understand this," she began,

pleased she sounded so normal. "You're our locum tenens."

He nodded. "Yes."

"You're not going to Colorado."

"Not in the immediate future." To be honest, Evan didn't want to spend his vacation in New Hope. As she'd said, he was giving up cool mountain streams, the soothing rustle of the aspens, weeks of solitude and soul-searching for a summer holiday of scorching heat, constant wind and miles of flat land where trees had to be pampered in order to grow.

If he hadn't owed Winston for his very career, if he hadn't looked upon him as a member of his own family, he would have dismissed this idea before it had become reality.

As things stood now, once he'd eliminated all of Marta's objections and secured her co-operation, he'd leave town faster than she could list all of the human body's organ systems.

Something glimmered in her eyes. "As a physician—"

"Internist," he supplied.

"I'm sure your vacation can't last indefinitely."

Now he understood why she seemed sure of herself. She thought she could wait him out.

"True, except I'm on a leave of absence." He didn't think it necessary to explain the specific terms he'd negotiated—a minimum of four weeks to a maximum of three months. A few weeks spent in New Hope would still give him plenty of time for relaxing in Colorado.

"It won't matter how long you fill in," she said.

"You're only scheduled for one day a week in the clinic. Even if you committed to a year, you won't be able to influence my decision."

He had a second ace up his sleeve. "Then Dr Campbell didn't tell you about my hours?" he asked innocently.

Her eyes narrowed. "No, he didn't."

"Because you've struggled without a doctor for so long, we thought you'd have a tremendous backlog of cases. So I'll be coming in every morning."

"Every morning?"

"Like clockwork," he said cheerfully. Daily contact was required for his plan to succeed.

Marta sank onto the chair, looking stunned. "Look," she said, "I'll be perfectly honest. I don't want you here."

"I gathered as much."

"No, really. I *don't* want you here."

"You don't have a choice."

She opened her mouth as if to speak, then cleared her throat and lifted the receiver. "This won't work. Joe will simply have to send someone else."

"You can try," he agreed, "but if you want a doctor, you're going to have to take me."

"Surely there's someone else available." She sounded almost frantic.

"Joe doesn't have anyone else to spare and no time to look for a replacement. Of your alternatives—me or no one at all—I'd like to think I'm the better of the two."

For a few seconds, she met his gaze. Then, as if she'd realized who the real losers would be—her patients—she dropped the receiver back in its cradle. "In other words, you're the lesser of two evils."

"It's a matter of perspective."

She squared her shoulders and stood. "You really are just like him, aren't you?"

Evan sensed she was referring to Winston, and not Joe. "I appreciate the compliment."

"It wasn't flattery. Manipulating people isn't an honorable trait."

"I haven't manipulated you."

"What would you call it when you meddle in order to get what you want?"

"I volunteered my expertise and your boss was smart enough to take advantage of my offer. He could have refused. I don't call that manipulation."

Marta walked toward the door. "But you knew he wouldn't turn you away."

"I gambled…and won. Otherwise I wouldn't be here."

"Where you're clearly not wanted."

He rose. "It dawned on me early this morning why you're fighting me tooth and nail."

"Could it be because you'll hound me continuously about my grandfather? That you'll spend every spare moment telling me what a great guy he is?" she asked sweetly.

Evan ignored her comments because she'd figured out his game plan. "You're worried because if I stick around, you'll change your mind."

Her jaw dropped. "How utterly ridiculous," she sputtered.

"Is it?" he asked.

She didn't answer—a telling sign in his opinion. When she spoke again, her voice was coolly professional.

"I'll bring the charts of the people you should see today. You can use my office."

"I don't want to inconvenience you—"

"Too late," she said shortly. "You already have."

She reached for the knob, but he knew if she left it would be a long time until he could safely continue this conversation. "Wait."

Marta hesitated. Turning to face him, she raised one eyebrow.

"This doesn't have to be difficult. For either of us."

"Oh, it won't be," she determined. "Because you'll have your patients and I'll have mine. Our conversations will be limited to medical topics—nothing personal. And my grandfather's name is hereby off-limits."

She was beautiful when she was angry. Her warning, however, didn't intimidate Evan. "Winston needs you."

She scoffed. "You can't make me feel guilty. He doesn't need anyone, least of all me."

"It's true," he insisted. "You need him, too. You just don't realize it yet."

"Spare me the psychoanalysis, Dr Gallagher. I'm not interested."

"It's common sense."

Marta turned the knob and opened the door. "Common sense or not, it appears we're at an impasse. I'm not including Winston Clay in my life and you're not leaving until I do. So I hope you don't have any long-term career plans because this part of Kansas will become beachfront property before I'll change my mind.

"Now, if you're truly here to work, shall we get started?"

Evan had pushed as far as he dared. For now. "By all means. But, Marta, I don't give up easily."

She stared at him for a long moment. "Neither do I."

"I will not let him get to me," Marta muttered as she jerked charts off the racks, starting with Monica Taylor's. "He'll do his job and I'll do mine. That's all."

Deep in her thoughts, she didn't notice the whisper of Ros's wheels coming behind her.

"It's not a good sign to hear you talking to yourself so early in the day," Ros said cheerfully. "I noticed a familiar Lexus parked outside."

"Don't remind me," Marta complained.

Ros glanced around. "So where is he?" She leaned forward. "On second thoughts, don't tell me where you stashed the body. I'd rather not know."

"He's in my office. Apparently he's wiggled his way into Dr Campbell's good graces and is now going to be our physician."

"Unbelievable. Do you think you can manage one day a week in his company?"

"It's worse than that. He's going to work every morning for who knows how long."

What a depressing thought. To be in the presence

of one of the all-time most handsome men and know his goal was only to be a thorn in her side—a constant reminder of things better left forgotten.

Why couldn't he be short, forty pounds overweight, balding, and have a face capable of curdling milk with one glance? At least then her hormones wouldn't add their two cents' worth to the situation.

"Great. Who do you want me to call first?" Ros had a list of patients with conditions requiring a physician's attention, but which weren't of an emergency nature. Rather than drive to Liberal, those people had asked to wait until the next time the doctor visited.

"Must you be so cheerful about this?"

Ros shrugged. "It'll be nice to have easy access to a physician for a change."

"I just wish it would have been someone else."

"Things have a way of working out," Ros said.

Marta groaned as she pulled the last chart. "Just what I needed. My secretary waxing philosophical."

"And all at no extra charge," Ros quipped.

Marta held the stack under Ros's nose. "Then I must be paying you too much. See if you can get in touch with these folks."

Ros, gifted with an ability to remember names, glanced at the tags and nodded. "Will do. I'll let you know in a few minutes."

Marta took the charts down the hall, grateful for the camaraderie she shared with Ros. She'd need someone to help get her through the upcoming weeks until Evan Gallagher faced facts and accepted defeat.

She found him in her office, studying her notebooks filled with diagnostic protocols.

"These cases are the most pressing," she said, dropping the files on her desk. "Ros will let us know as soon as they arrive."

He took the top folder. "Ricardo Rodriguez."

"He has a knot on his forehead about the size of a golf ball."

"Tumor?"

"It's probably a lipoma. He's had one excised before just like it, so he's not worried about it being cancerous. His son is getting married at the end of the summer and he doesn't want to have a lump on his face for the pictures."

Evan nodded. "OK. What about Maria Gonzales?"

"Thirty-year-old diabetic. Her last hemoglobin A1C test was way out of range. I thought it might be a good idea if you saw her."

"What about her blood glucose?"

"The few times I've checked it with the meter, it's been fine but, as you know, a finger-stick test only shows her current status. The A1C test indicates long-term compliance."

"Do you think she's cheating on her diet or just needs to adjust her insulin?"

"Both."

"All right." Evan opened the third chart. "What about Juanita Lopez?"

"Hypertension. She's thirty-five and developed high blood pressure about six months ago. She was taking oral contraceptives at the time, and so we discontinued them. Her BP dropped, but has steadily climbed again. It hasn't been below 150 over 100 for about six weeks."

"Have you done any urine studies? Catecholamines, metanephrines, creatinine?"

Marta shook her head. "Dr Laraby—he left before Dr Evans came on board—talked about doing those, but he never ordered them."

"We may do them now," Evan decided. "I'll know more after I examine her."

He closed the file and grabbed the last one. "Monica Taylor."

Marta drew a deep breath. "She's my biggest worry. She always presents with something serious, but I can't ever find anything wrong. She was in yesterday complaining of chest pain, but her ECG was normal. We sent a blood sample off for heart enzymes, but her results fell within the normal range."

He flipped through the records. "She comes in frequently with stomach upsets."

"Yes. Over-the-counter meds seem to help, but the one time I could talk her into having an upper GI, the X-ray was normal."

"Hmm," he said thoughtfully as he read through her notes. Marta waited for him to finish, noticing the combination of a woodsy cologne and soap surrounding him. Marta wanted to find fault with the pleasant scent, but couldn't.

"She certainly presents with a variety of problems," he finally said. "There's no rhyme or reason either."

"I know. I'm afraid I'm missing something."

"Her complaints seem straightforward. According to your documentation, you've checked her thoroughly. Maybe she's a hypochondriac."

"Maybe, which is why I wanted a physician's opinion."

He leaned back in his chair. "OK. We'll see how she is when she comes in today."

"Thanks."

"Can you explain how things work around here? Appointments, lab tests and all that?"

Marta relaxed. As long as they limited their conversations to medical issues, she could suffer his presence and come through this relatively unscathed. With any luck, he'd soon recognize the futility of waiting for her to open any discussions. He'd tire, then move on, and life for both of them would return to normal.

"About two-thirds of my patients come in for check-ups and monitoring—Coumadin, insulin, digoxin, cholesterol levels and blood pressures. Another third are minor emergencies—sore throats, gashes, an occasional broken arm."

"What about the major cases?" Evan asked.

"We have a scanner and a police-band radio in the office that connects us to the county emergency medical service. Our volunteer firemen are EMTs and we're lucky enough to also have one who worked as a paramedic in the city before coming back to New Hope. Between the two of us, we stabilize the patient before sending him on."

"Then you're on call all of the time?"

"More or less. It's generally quiet."

"But what happens when you leave town?" he pressed.

"As I said, we have a good crop of emergency

staff. They're experienced and know what they're doing.''

"I read through your protocol book. It's very thorough.''

She flushed under his praise. "Thanks. I tried to make it as comprehensive as possible. It's come in handy more than once.''

Ros appeared in the doorway. "Monica and Juanita are here. I haven't been able to reach the others, but I'll keep trying.''

"Thanks.'' Marta rose. "Are you ready?'' she asked Evan.

"You bet.''

For the next hour, Marta was forced to admire both Evan's medical skills and his manner with patients. What really surprised her was the way he greeted Juanita in Spanish, although he admitted he wasn't very fluent. Marta grudgingly gave him points for making the effort.

He ordered blood work and urine tests, making his request sound as if they were run-of-the mill procedures in order to keep Juanita from worrying about her elevated blood pressure before she left.

To Monica Taylor, Evan asked the same questions Marta had asked on previous occasions. That in itself was rather gratifying.

"Your heart is fine,'' he told the woman. "In fact, you're in excellent health.''

"Really?'' Monica seemed surprised. "Sometimes it feels like it's racing and then my chest hurts so bad I can't hardly breathe. Are you sure you can't find anything wrong with me?''

"I'm positive," he assured her. "Your pulse rate is fine, I don't hear any murmurs, the ECG doesn't show any arrhythmias, and your lungs are clear. Everything seems to be in working order."

She gave him a dubious look. "If you say so. What do I do if I get chest pain again?"

"By all means, come back," he told her as he ushered her through the door.

"Well, what do you think?" Marta asked him privately.

"She's in better shape than a lot of people her age. Does she, by any chance, have someone who checks on her periodically?"

"Not that I know of."

"Then all we can do is exactly what we've done today." Evan paused. "If she lives alone, she may be dwelling on the normal aches associated with growing older. If you think about any pain long enough, you can imagine the worst when it isn't so."

"You're right."

Evan smiled. "So rest easy. From what I can see, you've been thorough in your assessments. I'm impressed."

Her face warmed under his praise. "Thanks."

"And I'm not just saying it to flatter you," he continued. "Some of my med students aren't as observant as you are."

"Med students?" she asked.

He nodded. "St Margaret's is a teaching facility. They all come through my department at one time or another."

His department! Evan Gallagher wasn't a run-of-the-mill doctor if he held such an enviable position. His acting as a locum didn't make sense. He might be friends with Winston, but friendship only went so far.

"Who's next?" he asked.

"That's it for today," she informed him.

"You don't see patients this afternoon?"

She shook her head. "Not on Wednesdays. From September through May, I act as the district's school nurse. Since it's summer and school isn't in session, I take the afternoon off."

"Oh." He headed for the door. "If you should need me, I'm staying at the Lazy Daze Motel. Number Six. Any suggestions on a good place to eat?"

Marta almost felt sorry for Evan. She couldn't imagine having to eat the diner's simple food at every meal for weeks on end, especially when his palate was probably used to exotic fare like lobster and quiche. Yet, in spite of her grudging respect for the way he treated her patients, she couldn't bring herself to offer a home-cooked meal. He'd volunteered to spend his vacation in New Hope, and if he suffered from the lack of amenities then he had no one to blame but himself.

"The Steakhouse Grill is good."

"I'll try it," he said. "By the way, do you know of any apartments to rent?"

"There are a few complexes at the east end of town. They're not very fancy."

"As long as it has the basics, I don't care. Wait, I take that back. A comfortable mattress is a must."

"Bad back?" she asked, imagining him sprawled across a bed, wearing only a sheet that barely covered his hips.

"No. When you've spent as much time in bed as I have lately, comfort is a necessity."

Good heavens! Was he bragging about his exploits? Her distaste must have showed on her face, because he laughed.

"I know what you're thinking, and you're wrong. I caught hepatitis A from shellfish at a dinner party."

"I hope you fired the chef."

"I didn't hire him," he said ruefully. "I was wining and dining a prospective donor at an exclusive restaurant, trying to coax him and his wife into contributing to the new wing of St Margaret's."

She laughed. "Talk about making an impression."

He smiled. "I'd made the reservations based upon their recommendation. Naturally, they felt terrible when I got sick and they didn't."

"I'm sure."

"The evening wasn't a total loss. They made an extremely generous donation to compensate."

Marta wasn't surprised. Money had a way of easing guilt.

"But don't worry," he continued. "I'm not contagious. I just haven't regained my energy."

"Is that why you were going to Colorado? To recuperate?"

"Partly." He didn't offer any more information and although Marta's curiosity was aroused, she didn't ask any more questions. She'd already broken her rule about keeping their conversations strictly professional.

Evan's private life was none of her business. If she ventured there, she'd relax her guard and then, before she knew what had happened, she'd forget that he wasn't just a locum from nowhere who was here for a few weeks.

Developing a friendship with a man who enjoyed a close relationship with her grandfather was simply asking for trouble.

CHAPTER FOUR

FOR the next ten days, Marta wanted to find fault with Evan…and couldn't. He was efficient, highly skilled and polite to everyone, including her…and it was driving her to distraction.

On that Friday, Evan had just left for lunch and his usual afternoon off. Marta rummaged through her desk drawer in search of something to settle her stomach.

"Digging for lost treasure?"

Ros's familiar voice didn't stop Marta. "Very funny. Have you seen—?"

"No." Ros wheeled toward the desk.

Marta glanced up. "How can you say no? You don't know what I want."

"Yes, I do. Your stomach is on the warpath and you're looking for your usual solution."

"All right. I admit it," Marta grumbled, irritated at Ros's smug attitude and her ability to read her so accurately. "Have you seen my—?"

Ros held out an empty bottle. "Right here."

Marta frowned. "I just bought those."

"I know." The plastic container thudded against the trash can as she tossed it inside. "Can a person get addicted to antacids?"

"Oh, for heaven's sake." Marta rolled her eyes. "I'm not addicted."

"You're eating them like candy. I may only be a medical secretary, but it seems to me that if you need them that often, you have a real problem."

"I do. It's called Evan Gallagher."

"I can't imagine why. He's gorgeous, utterly fantastic to work with and—"

"Spare me your list of his sterling qualities. He's charmed you and everyone else in town. I'll bet if he'd ask for the moon, you'd do your best to give it to him."

Marta returned her attention to the drawer. Surely she could find a loose tablet floating around with the conglomeration of rubber bands, paper clips, staples, stamps and notepads.

"I live to serve," Ros said cheerfully.

"If he hadn't agreed to let you analyze his handwriting, you'd hold a far different opinion of the man."

"I asked because I thought he'd make an interesting character study," Ros said defensively. "Then maybe you'll see him as one of the good guys."

"Fat chance. I don't want to see him at all. I want him to leave town." Marta slammed the drawer closed and leaned back in her chair.

"No, you don't. He's been too valuable to have around and you know it. Look at what he's accomplished. He's adjusted Maria's insulin and convinced her to quit fudging on her diet. He's running tests on Mrs Lopez that I've never heard of, just so he can get a handle on her high blood pressure. Plus—"

"OK, OK. He's an adequate doctor to have around."

"Adequate? Why, he's fantastic. I didn't know doctors like him existed!"

"Let's not get carried away," Marta said, refusing to broadcast the high regard she held for his medical abilities. If her personal life wasn't linked to his, she'd worship the ground he walked on like everyone else.

He'd become a familiar sight as he pedaled around town on the mountain bike he'd purchased from The Cycle Center and had thoroughly charmed all who crossed his path. In fact, she wouldn't be surprised if the city council decided to build and name a bike trail after him.

Her personal life was definitely the problem. She could be discussing a patient when all of a sudden she'd notice his cologne, the way he stroked his chin with long, lean fingers, or the dimple in his cheek when he smiled. Awareness would strike like a bolt of lightning. Her knees would wobble until her brain began to function again and remind her of his true purpose for being in her clinic. She didn't have any business being attracted to a man who was literally making her life miserable without even trying.

"I don't know why you're tying yourself in knots over him. He's a friend of your grandad's. It's hardly a hanging offense."

"It should be," Marta snapped.

Ros shrugged. "I hate to say this, but you're acting childish…and chicken."

Marta opened her mouth to argue, then stopped. Ros was right. The insecurity, anger and frustration of the fifteen-year-old girl buried inside her had resurfaced after all these years. Marta had thought she'd laid those feelings to rest long ago, but apparently not.

She sighed, letting her shoulders droop. "Oh, Ros. I don't know what I'm going to do. The man makes me so nervous I could literally jump out of my skin."

"What does he do to set you on edge? He's so polite and calm, never raises his voice and is always friendly. As far as I can tell, he doesn't have a single irritating habit either."

"That's the problem. He's *too* nice." Without a few more faults to focus on, it was getting harder to justify her dislike of him.

Ros raised one eyebrow. "Then by all means, we should run him out of town. You get the tar and I'll find the feathers. Better yet, let's form a posse and lynch him!"

Marta threw Ros an exasperated glance. "You know what I mean."

"No," Ros said. "I don't. How can one be too nice?"

"You said it yourself. He's polite and personable, even when he shouldn't be." Marta thought of how last Friday Evan had hunted her down to ask a question about one of her referrals. She'd been so mesmerized by his long eyelashes and the luster of his eyes she'd lapsed into another momentary daydream. Unnerved by her lack of control, she'd told him to read the chart before she'd walked away. She would never, *ever* have said that to a physician, but she had, and to a man who'd probably forgotten more medical knowledge than she'd ever learned.

"You'd feel better if he yelled at you once in a while?"

"No. Yes. I don't know. I just want to see him... respond."

"Why? So you can call Dr Campbell and tell him how impossible Dr Gallagher is to work with?"

Marta felt a twinge of embarrassment. "All right. So the thought crossed my mind. I was more in hopes of him getting tired of the cold treatment and leaving on his own."

Unfortunately, she'd failed miserably at her own plan. She warmed to him on a regular basis and it took an extreme act of will to maintain her icy emotional distance. Their days had as many ups and downs as The Mamba roller-coaster ride at Worlds of Fun. He'd probably diagnosed her as having a case of terminal PMS.

Not that it mattered what he thought, she reminded herself crossly.

Ros shook her head. "I told you. He won't give up."

Marta cast a wry glance at Ros. "I'm convinced."

"OK. We've established that you want him to chew you out, but he's too polite. Now, tell Auntie Ros what the *real* problem is."

Marta's excuse sounded silly, even to herself. "It's nothing."

"Of course it's something, otherwise you wouldn't have bought enough antacid tablets to send the company stock prices soaring."

"It's irrational and ridiculous."

"Most fears often are."

Marta hesitated, trying to explain her turmoil when she didn't have the words. "We've talked, but he's strictly business. And if he *does* talk about other topics, they're always about general things, like the weather, or the price of gasoline."

"Isn't that what you wanted? If I remember, you declared your grandfather's name as off-limits."

Marta nodded. "I know, but even though Evan is playing by my rules, I feel like we're in a holding pattern, waiting for…something. Then, when I least expect it, after I've let down my guard, he'll move in for the proverbial kill and I won't have any defenses in place."

Ros slowly nodded. "I see. The question is, why do you need to protect yourself?"

Because Winston Clay drained every ounce of my self-esteem out of me, she silently answered.

"The first time I saw Winston Clay," Marta said quietly, forcing herself to remember, "he yelled at me for having the audacity to appear in his office. I'd never felt so insignificant, so *unimportant*, in my life. When I walked out, I was bound and determined to become someone just as important and successful as he was."

"Oh, Marta." Distress filled Ros's voice. "After knowing you all these years, I had no clue what drove you to work so hard…"

Marta shrugged. "Yeah, well, I don't like to talk about it."

Ros fell silent, and when she spoke her voice had softened. "I understand why your stomach is always churning, but you're going to have to get past this.

The situation with your grandfather is eating away at you and it isn't healthy, physically or emotionally.''

''I know.'' However, forgiving Winston was easier said than done.

''If I can tell you're gobbling those...'' Ros motioned to the empty bottle in the trash ''...more often than you should, don't you suppose Dr Gallagher has noticed, too?''

Marta thought of how, just that morning, he'd come upon her slipping a tablet in her mouth. After seeing him frown, she'd expected him to comment, but he hadn't. Instead, his expression had cleared and he'd only raised an eyebrow as he'd questioned if she'd received the latest lab results on Juanita Lopez.

Oh, he definitely knew the effect he was having on her.

''He's noticed,'' Marta admitted. ''He just hasn't said anything.''

Ros became thoughtful. ''By worrying yourself sick, you're giving your grandfather control over you.''

The truth seemed to hit Marta right between her eyes. On that fateful afternoon, she'd vowed her grandfather would never have the power or the opportunity to hurt her again. Physical distance had taken care of the opportunity, but even after years of trying to block him out of her mind, she still struggled against the power of his rejection.

''You're also approaching this from the wrong angle,'' Ros added. ''You've gone on the defensive. Maybe you should switch sides.''

''You mean...?''

"Confront Dr Gallagher," Ros instructed. "Don't wait for him to mention the subject. Tell him what you told me and get it out in the open once and for all."

"I can't," Marta said flatly.

"You don't have a choice. Unless you prefer buying your antacids by the case instead of the bottle."

"He'll repeat everything I say to Winston. Then *that man* will know…" A lump formed in her throat. *How badly he hurt me*, she finished silently.

Ros's expression turned to one of sympathy. "This is hard for you, I know, but you can't go on like this."

Marta knew she couldn't. Which was why she had to get Evan Gallagher out of her life.

"So," Ros continued, somewhat triumphantly, "I've decided to help matters roll along. Someone has to save you from yourself."

Marta narrowed her eyes. "What did you do?"

"I invited Dr Gallagher to Charlie's birthday barbecue tonight."

Marta considered this. "Not a problem. Half the town shows up. I won't even see him—"

"Oh, yes, you will. Because he's going as *your* guest."

"What?"

The thought of bringing him to a community gathering was both heady and frightening. She'd be the envy of every single woman there. She'd also be a nervous wreck.

"You're going to pick him up at six-fifteen," Ros continued.

Marta shook her head. "I can't."

"Why not? Are you going with Del?"

"No. He's seeing Christina these days."

"I never understood why you two broke up."

"He wanted more out of our relationship than I could give," Marta replied. "I just couldn't connect with him on a level above friendship."

Sadly enough, Del was the second man she'd disappointed because she hadn't reciprocated his feelings. Some would say she was foolish to hold out for a guy who caused her heart to sing or her blood to hum through her veins, but she wanted electricity. She wanted sparks. Truthfully, she wanted a forest fire.

Maybe there was something wrong with her.

There definitely was, she thought wryly. Crossed wires had to account for her pulse to race, her hormones to shift into overdrive and her whole body to sizzle with awareness while in the presence of Evan Gallagher—a man totally unsuitable for her.

"By the way, are Rachel and Amy coming?" Ros asked.

"Yes, but they're not sure of their schedule, so I'll meet them at the party."

"Then you're free to take Evan," Ros insisted, returning to the subject Marta thought had been dropped. "The man would probably die for a chance to eat something other than what the Grill or the Pizza Place serves. If I were him, I'd kiss the feet of anyone who gave me an alternative to steak and pizza."

A tiny measure of guilt niggled at her. While both restaurants served good food, a steady diet of their cuisine grew old rather fast. If Evan had been anyone else, she'd have invited him for a few home-cooked meals long ago.

But could she spend an evening with him, an evening where she didn't have their work to act as a buffer? An evening where she thought only of him as a companion and not as Winston's errand boy?

On the other hand, the idea of beating him to the punch—putting him on the defensive rather than vice versa—had its own merit.

"I'll think about it."

"Don't take too long," Ros warned. "He's expecting you at six-fifteen. It's almost one-thirty now."

"I said I'd think about it."

Ros studied her. "And you won't forget?"

How could she? "I won't forget."

Apparently satisfied by the half-hearted promise, Ros quietly steered her chair down the hallway, leaving Marta alone with her thoughts.

Maybe Ros had a good idea. Waiting for things to happen wasn't in her nature. She'd learned the importance of going after what she wanted, full steam ahead.

In fact, taking Evan to the Zindel barbecue—and bringing him home—could be her perfect opportunity to reach a compromise. She was willing to give him the proverbial inch in this situation, but not an entire mile. He certainly couldn't expect her to confront the ghosts of her past overnight.

She rubbed the ache in the pit of her stomach. It was taking far too much energy to maintain her anger toward him when he wasn't the one who deserved it. She'd fallen into the trap of attacking the messenger because she didn't like the message, and it was time to stop.

She rubbed her eyes and let her shoulders sag. OK, she'd take Evan to the party. She'd also suffer through his speech of how wonderful Winston Clay was and explain how too much water had passed under the bridge for a reconciliation to take place.

Then she could continue with her life and he could move on with his.

If he had any sense, he'd put this fool's notion of helping Winston out of his head and move on with his life.

Evan stretched out on his bed in his motel room and clicked through the television channels in rapid succession. He'd seen enough of the programming to be thankful he was normally too busy to watch TV on a regular basis. He'd also rented nearly every video offered by the local grocery store, which wasn't a real accomplishment considering their very limited selection.

Part of his problem lay in that this was his first *real* vacation in his entire life and he didn't know what to do with himself. As a kid, money had been spent on necessities like food, not luxuries like vacations. As soon as he'd been able, he'd worked every summer, intent on saving his earnings rather than spending them. His free time as a med student, an intern and then as a resident had passed by in much the same way—working to pay off his debts.

However, if he'd had an inkling of how he'd spend the better part of his dream vacation in a run-down motel instead of a luxury condominium, he'd have thought twice about taking on the role of peacemaker between Winston and his long-lost granddaughter.

It served him right for being so cocky. His success had gone to his head and he'd thought he could waltz into Marta's office, say a few charming words, then be on his merry way.

Hardly.

And yet his days hadn't been a total waste. His physical stamina had grown, thanks to his daily routine of bicycling around town, and he enjoyed his part-time duties at the clinic. Working "in the trenches" provided a change of pace from his teaching and other administrative responsibilities.

After spending so much of his time wining and dining potential donors for St Margaret's many projects, it was refreshing to return to practicing medicine. He'd missed treating patients as people rather than as textbook cases. During his bout of hepatitis, the questions in his mind concerning his current career path had refused to be silenced any longer.

His recuperation/vacation was supposed to help him find his answers. Instead, he'd merely shoved his problems into the background and accepted a completely different set.

On the surface, it appeared as if he wasn't making any headway with Marta, but he knew he was. She'd thawed considerably from her initial icy disdain, although occasionally, as if she realized he was the enemy, she would slip back into her Ice Princess mode.

He'd abided by her rule of not mentioning Winston's name, knowing she'd expected him to break it at the first opportunity. From the way she gobbled down those antacids, her carefree attitude was only an act.

In a way, he felt guilty about the role he'd assumed. He'd played this game before—hammering out a compromise between two equally stubborn people. This time there was more at stake than the size of a tax deduction. Never had he encountered a person whose health had suffered because of the subtle pressure he exerted.

And never had he so intensely yearned to take someone into his arms, hold her close and whisper assurances that everything would work out for the best. Afterwards, well, he knew it wouldn't take much for nature to take its course.

Her light scent had become as familiar to him as his own. The woman didn't even have to be in the same room for him to want to yank off her shapeless scrub suits, unclasp her hair and run his hands through every strand, and bury himself deep inside her.

None of which were remotely possible. Marta might tolerate being in the same room with him, but not much else. Even if her attitude changed, he wasn't about to repay Winston by having an affair with his granddaughter, no matter how delightful the prospect might be.

Maybe he should call the whole thing off, he thought. Before he totally lost all good sense.

As attractive as the idea sounded, he knew he wouldn't quit. He was already past the point of no return and his instincts promised a breakthrough soon.

In fact, tonight's birthday party could present the

moment he'd been waiting for so patiently. He knew
Ros had been behind the invitation and he wondered
how she'd convince Marta to act as his chauffeur.
Had anyone other than the feisty receptionist cooked
up this scheme, he wouldn't have held much hope for
its success. Tempered steel lay underneath Ros's
easygoing manner and he couldn't imagine Marta de-
nying her anything.

He glanced at his watch. One forty-five. He had at
least four and a half hours before he had to get ready
for tonight's party. The walls suddenly seemed to
close in on him and he bounded off the bed, clicking
off the television at the same time. Soaking in a pool
sounded like pure heaven, even if he had to compete
with every kid in New Hope for a lap lane.

Having made his decision, he quickly exchanged
his clothes for his swimsuit. The telephone interrupted
his search for a pair of athletic shorts and a T-shirt,
but he didn't mind. Talking to someone—*anyone*—
was better than being alone with his thoughts. With
any luck, it was the landlord of the Land's End apartment complex, informing him of an unexpected va-
cancy.

"Evan? Dr Gallagher?"

The familiar feminine voice caught him by surprise, but he'd rather hear Marta on the other end of
the line than George Keating, no matter how badly
he wanted to leave his six-legged roommates behind.

"What's up?" he asked, hiding his eagerness for a
live conversation behind nonchalance. It was a good
thing she couldn't see the grin on his face.

"We have a young man in his twenties who has a problem."

"OK. How serious is it?"

"It's not life-threatening," she assured him. "He's breathing and I don't see any blood. Whatever it is, he's terribly worried."

"Then could you—?"

She interrupted. "He insists on having you—and you alone—examine him. Are you free?"

Was he free? Wild mustangs couldn't keep him from this unscheduled trip to the clinic.

"I'll be there in twenty minutes," he promised, tucking the phone between his ear and shoulder so he could rummage through the dresser drawers.

"Can you make it sooner?"

His heart skipped a beat. Her voice seemed… softer. "I'll be there as soon as I pull some clothes on."

The pregnant pause in his ear made him smile. Clearly her thoughts weren't as pure as newly fallen snow. "I was on my way to the pool."

Her brief "oh" sounded like a squeak, then she cleared her throat. "Come as soon as you can."

"I'll be there in ten."

He made it in nine and a half.

If the look on Marta's face hadn't been so serious, he would have teased her about meeting him at the door. Before he could say a word, she thrust a slim folder into his hand.

"Thanks for coming back," she apologized. "I hope we didn't ruin your afternoon plans."

He shrugged. "Spur-of-the-moment stuff. Nothing

that can't be done another day. So who's our patient?''

''James Carter. He's twenty-four and works at one of the cattle ranches. His vitals are fine, but his BP is up. Probably due to nerves, because he literally can't sit still.''

''And he's here because…?'' His voice faded and he raised an eyebrow, waiting for her to fill in the blank.

She shrugged. ''He won't give me a clue. It's clearly something he'd rather share with another male. I wouldn't have bothered you, but he's terribly shy. Considering how worried he acts, I hated to make him suffer through the weekend.''

''Good thing I'm in town.''

Her face turned pink, and she looked away, but didn't answer him directly. Expecting her to voice her gratitude for his presence was too much to ask for at this stage in the game. At least she hadn't denied it.

''He's waiting in room two,'' she said.

''I'll call if I need anything.''

''I'll be here,'' she promised.

Evan stepped into the room. ''James?'' he asked.

The young man sitting on the exam table, his skin tanned from years of exposure to the sun, nodded. ''Folks call me Jim.''

''Jim it is. Marta says that you specifically asked to see me.'' Evan grinned. ''It's nice to have a patient request me by name. What seems to be the problem?''

''No seemin' about it,'' James answered. ''I noticed this here lump a few weeks after a steer rammed into me." He pointed to his genitals. "It hasn't gone away, so I figgered it was time to see a doctor."

"Good idea." Evan motioned for Jim to drop his jeans and lie down on the exam couch while he tugged on a pair of extra-large latex gloves. A second later, he palpated the man's testicles.

"Does this hurt?"

Jim shook his head. "No."

"Do you have pain anywhere else? Say, in your back?"

"Naw."

"Have you developed a cough or anything that you might think was a cold?"

Once again, Jim shook his head.

Evan quickly checked his ankles for edema and found nothing. All good signs.

"Is it cancer?" Jim's voice quivered and his hands tightened into fists.

Evan replaced the sheet before stripping off his gloves. "It could be," he said kindly, "but I really can't say at this point. I'm going to arrange for an appointment with a urologist. Do you have a preference as to which one you want me to call?"

"Naw. Never had trouble with my plumbing before. What'll he do?"

"He'll request lab tests and probably a sonogram," Evan began. "He may even require surgery to make a definitive diagnosis." If the urologist suspected testicular cancer, as Evan did, Jim would undergo an orchidectomy where the testicle was removed so it could be examined microscopically.

Jim's brown eyes widened further. "Never thought

I'd end up a steer instead of a bull. Seems kind of weird, considering I'm right handy with a knife when it comes to beef.''

"Let's not get ahead of ourselves," Evan said calmly.

"I've always wanted to have kids.''

"You won't be sterile unless both testicles are removed. Some men choose to donate to a sperm bank beforehand, but the urologist will advise you on your options. As I said, let's not cross that bridge until we get there.''

He clapped Jim on the back. "Why don't you get dressed and I'll make your appointment?''

Evan found Marta in their closet storeroom, rearranging their supplies. "Who's the best urologist in the area?''

"Dr Tubman. His number's on my Rolodex.''

A few minutes later, he was standing in Marta's office, speaking directly to Bill Tubman and trying to keep his mind on Jim Carter rather than on Marta's residual scent. "I have a young man with a possible testicular cancer. I know it's Friday afternoon, but could you work him in today?''

"If he can get here before four," Bill told him.

The cheap clock on Marta's wall always ran about fifteen minutes fast. Right now, it read three p.m. He held his hand over the phone to speak to her. "How long would it take to get to Tubman's office?''

"Thirty minutes. Twenty if you want to risk a speeding ticket.''

Evan spoke into the receiver. "It'll be close, but he'll be there.''

"It's not good, is it?" Marta asked as soon as he disconnected the call.

"A non-painful lump in a healthy male in his twenties often indicates testicular cancer. If so, he's fortunate because he's not showing any signs of a spreading metastasis. No back pain, no edema in his legs, no respiratory problems."

"Would you refresh my memory on how they'll tell what stage he's in?"

"First they'll do a scrotal ultrasound and blood work. A beta HCG—"

"The pregnancy hormone," she supplied.

"Yes. Plus others. If those are positive, they'll remove the affected testicle. Then, depending on what the CT scan of his abdomen, pelvis and chest shows, they'll be able to tell if or how far the disease has spread."

"And the treatment?"

"Surgery and chemotherapy are used. But, like I told him, let's not jump to conclusions. He may be one of the really lucky ones and it's just a benign epidermoid cyst."

"Let's hope so."

Evan drew a deep breath. "I'd better tell him Dr Tubman will see him as soon as he arrives."

Back inside the exam room, he informed Jim of his immediate appointment. "Don't panic because things are moving fast," he said. "Dr Tubman wanted to get some of the tests in progress before the weekend arrives. Drive carefully, because wrecking your car won't help matters."

Jim managed a grin. "I don't guess it would."

As soon as he'd gone, Evan faced Marta. "I'm really glad you called me. Maybe Jim's weekend won't be quite so stressful. Not knowing can sometimes be worse than facing the truth."

"I agree." She hesitated. "By the way, I understand Ros told you about Charlie's party."

Her serious tone made him wary and he wondered where the conversation would lead. "Yes, she did."

She took a deep breath and her words sounded rushed. "I'll be by to pick you up at six-fifteen. If that's OK with you?"

CHAPTER FIVE

MARTA waited, hoping Evan would respectfully decline to attend and knowing he wouldn't.

If he was surprised by her comment, he didn't show it. Instead, a slow smile spread across his face. "Yeah, sure," he drawled. "Six-fifteen. I'll be ready."

Sweet Betsy, she was committed to Ros's unholy plan. Why did everyone feel as if they had to meddle in her life? "It's casual, so dress accordingly."

Unbidden, her mental picture of him wearing a pair of swimming trunks appeared. Considering the fit of his trousers and the way the fabric molded itself to his thighs, her imagination couldn't be too far off the mark.

He nodded. "Casual I can do. Dressy is a problem."

She hadn't thought about it before, but his comment explained why he didn't wear dress shirts and ties. One didn't usually pack formal wear for a vacation trip.

"We'll be outside, so it'll be hot. They usually serve ribs, so it'll be messy, too."

He gave her a thumbs-up signal. "Hot and messy. Got it."

"Don't feel obligated," she said. "If you have

other plans…'' For pity's sake, what was she doing? Trying to give him an excuse to stay away?

Yes, she was, she admitted. Because, as much as she wanted to clear the air and send him packing, part of her didn't like the idea.

Skeletons were better left in their closets.

''I didn't have any other plans. Pardon me for asking, though,'' he said, his face expressionless, ''but you're not going to abandon me in some deserted field, are you?''

His teasing tone brought a wave of heat spreading upwards from her neck. ''I won't leave you to fend for yourself. I promise.''

Evan's gaze met hers and she saw the twinkle in those dark depths. ''Then I'll see you in a little while. Unless there are more patients waiting?''

She laughed. ''Haven't you had enough for today? You're supposed to be resting and recreating.''

''The Lazy Daze isn't exactly the holiday resort of the Midwest.''

She couldn't imagine staying more than a day at the motel, and then only under duress. To think he'd suffered for more than a week… Once again a twinge of guilt over her rudeness struck her. ''No luck finding an apartment?''

He shook his head. ''I was hoping the manager would have called by now, but he hasn't.''

''Too bad,'' she said sincerely.

''What? No comment about how it's a sign from God to hit the road?''

Once again Marta's skin warmed, as if she'd received an instant sunburn. Before her talk with Ros, she would have offered that very suggestion, but she'd since vowed to turn over a new leaf. "No comment."

Then, while she still had him flummoxed, she made an offer that a few hours ago would have caused her tongue to snap off its rollers. "If you don't want to go back—"

"I don't."

She smiled at his vehemence. "Feel free to hang around here for a while. Ros and I aren't expecting any patients, so we'll spend our last hour getting ready for Monday."

"If I help, we'll finish in half the time."

"Since when do doctors sweep floors and take out the trash?"

"Hey, I'm desperate. Besides, I've cleaned floors before. I worked in a grocery store when I was fifteen, stocking shelves and doing whatever odd jobs the manager asked me to do."

"Really?" How could a young man born with the proverbial silver spoon in his mouth have taken such a lowly position? She'd have expected him to start with a job more prestigious, like a bank vice-president.

"Of course I would never have gotten hired, but I was tall for my age and I fudged on my birth date."

"You're kidding. You lied?"

"It wasn't actually a lie. The ink smeared and the manager thought it was a five instead of a six. My parents and I were desperate for the income—my dad had been laid off—so I didn't correct his false impression. That one number let me work more hours."

Evan's comments had not only raised more questions but had also altered Marta's perceptions of his background. Perhaps she had more in common with Evan than she'd originally thought.

"In that case," she said lightly, "if you want to get started on the trash…? The Dumpster's out back."

He headed for the first room.

"And don't forget to wear gloves," she called.

He gave her a sassy salute, but obeyed.

As he'd promised, they made a swift end to their chores before locking the doors and going their separate ways.

Marta agonized over her clothes, wishing for advice from Amy, her fashion-conscious stepsister. After discarding a pair of trousers and a cotton blouse as being too hot for the hundred-degree heat, and a pair of shorts and tank top as being inappropriate, she settled on a floral print sundress and sandals. She let her hair hang loosely around her shoulders, although she slipped on a baseball cap to keep the wind from tangling her curls during the drive to Charlie's place via the Hazy Daze Motel.

She pulled into the parking stall in front of the door marked "SIX". Before she could slide out from behind the steering-column, Evan walked outside.

He stood on the sidewalk, giving her vehicle the once-over while she reciprocated. My, but he looked good. Breathtaking, in fact. A pair of navy twill shorts covered muscular thighs and a white polo shirt with a sporting logo stitched on the right side stretched across a broad chest. She couldn't think of a single male in town who could compare.

"I didn't tell you before, but nice wheels."

She heard the note of admiration in his voice and felt a twinge of embarrassment over how close she'd come to driving over his feet. "Thanks. Hop in."

To her surprise, he reached for the bar over the door and hauled himself inside without so much as a grunt. She reversed while he fastened his seat belt.

"I hadn't figured you with a Wrangler," he admitted. "A van maybe, but definitely not a Jeep."

"Between the snow in winter and the mud in the spring, I needed something with a four-wheel drive."

She accelerated as they left town. The wind whistled past and she had to turn her head to hear him speak.

"How far out of town is this barbecue?"

She pointed to a side road directly ahead. "We're almost there. Hang on. The road's a little bumpy."

She gripped the steering-wheel, suddenly conscious of his attention straying to her bare arms before moving on to her bare shoulders. Those two little straps holding up her dress suddenly seemed far too flimsy and unstable.

She was also aware of how this was the first time he'd seen her in clothes tailored to her form rather than the baggy uniforms she wore at work. She'd chosen not to wear her strapless bra and now she felt as if she could see right through the cotton fabric of her bodice to the skin underneath.

Seeing a huge hole in the sanded road directly ahead, she downshifted to avoid it. As she depressed the clutch with her left foot, she felt the hem of her dress ride high above her knee.

She should have worn those trousers after all.

And yet a quick glance at him showed the masculine appreciation on his face. She was woman enough to enjoy it.

"Looks like there's a big crowd," he commented as she guided her Wrangler through a maze of cars before she parked in a place where she wouldn't get blocked in.

"Charlie's family always throws a big party. They provide the beef and the guests provide the rest." She opened the door to slide out as gracefully as possible, noticing that once again Evan simply jumped over the door.

Oh, to have been granted long legs!

"Could you hand me the ice chest and that sack with his present?" she asked, nodding toward the back seat as she removed her cap and fluffed her hair with her fingers.

Evan obliged. "I hate to admit this, but I'm starving already."

She grinned. "Me, too. Come on. I'll drop these off and then we can mingle."

She introduced Evan to Charlie Zindel, the birthday boy and guest of honor, watching for Evan's reaction to the thirteen-year-old who was sitting in an easy chair and had peach fuzz covering his scalp.

"How do you do, Charlie?" he asked soberly, shaking his hand.

"Pretty good. Tired."

Charlie's mother, a blonde in her late thirties, broke

in. "He just came back from Camp Hope and I'm afraid he overdid it while he was away."

"I've heard about Camp Hope. It's here in Kansas, isn't it?"

Charlie nodded. "Near Great Bend."

"I don't need to ask if you had a great time," Evan said, smiling down at him.

"It was wonderful."

"Too wonderful," his mother, Lynette, added. "He's been exhausted all day. We wanted to postpone the party, but he insisted it go on."

"Absolutely," Evan declared. "You can't miss celebrating your first day as a teenager."

Charlie grinned. "No, sir. I can't." He glanced at his mother. "Don't worry, Mom. I know when I need to rest."

"Let's hope so," she scolded gently. "Now, you two, just make yourselves at home."

"We will," Marta promised. She led Evan through the crowd toward the tables loaded with birthday gifts and placed her package wrapped in vintage-car paper on top of a flat white box. Next she headed for the tables loaded with food, already finding it difficult to hear over the music blaring out of strategically placed speakers. Conversations in both English and Spanish flowed around her and she introduced Evan to everyone she met, including Walter, the county's paramedic, Frank, one of the EMTs, and the rest of the volunteer firemen.

"I've died and gone to heaven," Evan murmured in her ear.

"Why?" Marta stared at him, surprised to see the look of wonderment on his face.

He pointed. "The food. All that delicious *home-made* food."

Marta smiled as she placed her dish of spaghetti salad next to a bowl of cucumbers swimming in a vinegar dressing. "Withdrawal symptoms?"

"You don't know how boring restaurant fare can get. Or how quickly."

She pulled him aside. "Yeah, well, be careful of Minerva's bean concoction. It'll kill you."

"It looks good."

"Appearances can be deceiving. Eat it at your own risk. On the other hand, if you can get a taste of Juanita's chili Rellenos, you're in for a real treat."

She steered him toward the stock tank where soft drinks lay nestled in melting ice. He fished a cola out of the frigid water while she selected an orange soda.

Evan downed his in no time. "I'm curious about this birthday party," he said, tossing his empty can into the bin designated for recycling. "Somehow I'd expected Charlie to be older. Like an adult. I presume he has leukemia?"

She moved toward a few vacant chairs near a cottonwood and sat. "Acute lymphocytic. When Charlie was first diagnosed, the whole town rallied around the family. We raised money to help pay for his medical expenses and everyone waited with bated breath when he went in for his tests.

"To keep Charlie's—and their—spirits up, the Zindels began hosting a barbecue for his birthday. It became a symbol of hope to everyone. To Charlie, it was a milestone to reach.''

"Great idea.''

She nodded. "Of course, the possibility always exists of each year's bash being the last, but we've had three of these so far. A few months ago the doctors said he was in remission, so this year's party is extra special.''

"Where does he go for treatment?''

"M.D. Anderson.''

He nodded. "It's one of the best hospitals in the country.''

"Worth every penny,'' she agreed.

A flurry of voices and a high-pitched squeal caught her attention. Marta turned her head to see who had caused the commotion and saw her two stepsisters, Rachel and Amy, coming toward them.

"There you are,'' Amy called out. "We've been looking all over for you.''

Evan watched the three women embrace. He'd done his homework and knew the short, bubbly reddish-blonde was Amy, the youngest. The tallest of the three, Rachel, had brown hair and appeared more reserved than her sibling but equally friendly.

"We just got here,'' Marta said. "I was afraid you two weren't coming.''

Amy was aghast. "Miss Charlie's birthday? Not a chance.''

"At least you're staying until Sunday,'' Marta declared. "Did you pass your classes, Amy? And, Rachel, how's your new boss working out?''

Rachel rolled her eyes, but the love on her face

said that she didn't mind Marta's grilling. "We're fine, but I'm disappointed, sis. Your manners are slipping." She inclined her head in Evan's direction.

"Oh." Marta turned toward Evan. "Rachel, Amy, I'd like you to meet Dr Gallagher."

Rachel raised one eyebrow. "*Evan* Gallagher?"

Evan stuck out his hand. "Yes. Pleased to meet you."

"Likewise."

Before he knew what was happening, Rachel and Amy each took an arm and began escorting him toward the stock tank.

"You look a little parched," Amy said.

"I'm all right," he said, glancing over his shoulder at Marta.

She shrugged her shoulders. "I could use another drink. I'll go with you."

Rachel shook her head. "You've had him all to yourself and now it's our turn. Besides, you'd better save us a few chairs so we'll have a place to sit. Don't worry, we'll take good care of Evan. I'll bring you an orange soda."

Before he could object, Evan found himself being marched away.

"Why are you here?" Amy asked without preamble.

He knew she wasn't referring to the picnic. "To talk Marta into meeting her grandfather."

Rachel nodded. "We thought so. She mentioned your name after you phoned several weeks ago. I'm surprised you had the nerve to come in person."

"I'm only trying to reunite the two of them. There's nothing sinister about that."

"He's going to hurt her again," Amy predicted.

Evan shook his head. "No, he's not. He wants this reconciliation more than you can possibly imagine."

"Did she tell you they met before?" Rachel interrupted. At his nod, she continued. "It didn't go well. Marta never explained, although I'm guessing he tossed her out on her ear. She pretended it didn't matter, but it did. It still does. I especially feel bad because I'm the one who encouraged her to contact him in the first place."

"Really?"

Rachel nodded. "We'd worked everything out. She sneaked away from our motel one afternoon while our dad visited with some business people. She went to Mr Clay's office all excited and hopeful, but when she came back she was different. Harder, more driven. We love our sister, Dr Gallagher, and we don't want to see her hurt again."

"I understand. Believe me, hurting Marta is the last thing Winston wants to do."

The two women looked at each other in silent communication. Finally, Rachel spoke. "If you really mean that…"

"I do," he said.

The two exchanged glances again. "Then we'll help you as much as we can," Rachel finished.

The tension in his shoulders slowly faded. "You won't regret it."

"I certainly hope not," Amy said sweetly. "Keep

in mind, if you or Mr Clay cause her grief, there won't be any place you can hide from either of us.''

He grinned at her threat. ''I'll keep it in mind. You two wouldn't happen to know who sent the anonymous newspaper clipping to Winston several months ago, would you?''

Rachel sighed as she stared at her sister. ''Don't tell Marta, but we did it.''

''You?'' he asked, incredulous. ''After what you just put me through?''

''We weren't sure Winston cared about her,'' Rachel defended. ''We never knew what happened between them years ago, but we thought Mr Clay deserved a second chance.''

''We sent the article,'' Amy added, ''then waited to see what Winston would do. If he ignored it...'' she shrugged, ''...we'd let the whole thing drop. On the other hand, we thought it was worth the gamble to find out if he'd had a change of heart.''

''You're here, so it's safe to assume he has good intentions,'' Rachel finished. ''We're suckers for a happy ending.''

Evan shook his head. ''You two are something else.''

Amy grinned. ''Aren't we, though?''

''I'm not a psychologist,'' Rachel said, ''but I believe Marta's made herself indispensable to fill a void in her life. After Marta's mom—our stepmom—died, Marta kept us together when our dad fell apart. I guess losing two wives was more than he could handle.''

''Anyway,'' Amy interrupted, ''we're hoping her

grandfather isn't the hard-hearted ogre she believes him to be. If we made a mistake with our meddling this time..."

"Bringing those two together isn't a mistake," Evan stated. "You'll see."

"We hope so," Amy declared.

They'd reached the tank and Evan pulled another cola and an orange drink out of the ice.

"How long are you staying?" Rachel asked, popping the top on her can.

"I haven't made any definite plans, although I'll probably leave by August." He hoped six more weeks would be ample enough time to negotiate a truce.

"You're not interested in relocating to New Hope permanently?"

"I have my job in Dallas. To be honest, I need a faster pace."

"We understand." Before they reached the tree where Marta was waiting with a frown directed toward her sisters, Rachel squeezed his hand. "Good luck," she said softly.

"Thanks." He had a feeling he was going to need it.

Marta was relieved the three of them had returned so quickly. They wouldn't have had time to discuss anything at great length, although she suspected they'd thrown their support in his ring. They'd never minced words or held back their opinion about her relationship with her surviving family member, so they obviously saw Evan's presence as an answer to their prayer.

Amy sank into the chair beside Marta. "See, we brought your Dr Gallagher back safe and sound."

"And what stories did you manage to spin while you were gone?"

Rachel dismissed Marta's question with a brisk wave of one hand. "Spinning stories? Why, everything we told him was true."

Marta sighed and she avoided meeting Evan's gaze. "I was afraid of that."

Amy patted her hand. "We only have your best interests at heart. Oh, would you look at Del? I'd say there's romance in the air."

Marta glanced in the direction Amy had indicated. The familiar tall, lanky fellow had his arms around Christina and his lips plastered to hers. Both were clearly unconcerned about their audience. Her lack of response to seeing Del with another woman only emphasized the rightness of her decision to break off their relationship.

"Golly, Marta," Amy said, "you and Del were an item for so long, I thought for sure—"

"It doesn't pay for you to think," Marta quipped. "We wanted different things."

"Humph." Rachel crossed her arms. "At this rate, we're never going to be in your wedding party."

Marta hoped Evan would attribute the sudden rosiness of her skin to the sun and not embarrassment. Why point out her lack of romantic interests to a man who probably entertained a different woman every night of the month? "Yeah, but you won't have to buy a fancy dress so think of all the money you're saving.''

''Just so you'll know, we *want* to spend our salaries on dresses,'' Amy declared. ''I'm willing to eat peanut-butter-and-jelly sandwiches for a month. Which means, sister, dear, *get with the program*!''

Two young men, classmates of Amy and Rachel, sauntered by. ''Hey, you two,'' they said. ''Don't you know you're supposed to visit with everybody? We have a lot of catching up to do.''

Amy jumped to her feet and Rachel followed suit. ''See you around, sis,'' Amy said. Winking at Evan, she added, ''And don't wait up for us.''

''Speak for yourself,'' Rachel commented, bestowing a huge smile on the taller of the two men.

A moment later, Evan and Marta were alone. Relatively alone, considering the hordes of people making their way to form a line for the buffet.

''Seems like your sisters are eager for you to tie the knot,'' Evan commented.

''Tell me about it,'' she said glumly. ''I wish they'd pay as much attention to their own love lives as they do to mine.''

''They probably want you to be happy.''

''I'm happy now.''

''You know what I mean.''

She sighed. ''I know. Rachel wants a niece or nephew spoil and Amy thinks I'm lonely.''

''Are you? Lonely, that is?''

''I'm too busy to be lonely.''

''I could use a few extra hours in my day, too,'' he said, ''but there are times when I'm lonely.''

She couldn't believe it. "You're kidding. After hobnobbing with the wealthiest people of Dallas, escorting their beautiful daughters to ritzy events, you surely have run across someone you wanted regularly in your life."

"I did," he admitted. "Jill had two kids and we got along great."

"What happened?"

"Her ex came back to town, promised he'd delegate more of his work, cut down on the number of his overseas trips and be there for them."

"And she bought it?" She was incredulous.

"Yeah. I didn't think their relationship would work either, but she was willing to risk it. They've been together for three years and it appears he's doing everything he'd promised. He's home every night and every weekend, and doesn't take any trips except in the summer when she and their two girls can join them. Jill's expecting baby number three in December."

"Hey, you two." Ros wheeled her way toward them on the sidewalk and motioned them forward. "If you don't get in line, there won't be anything left."

Evan jumped to his feet and grabbed Marta by the hand. "Come on. I'm not about to miss out on home cooking."

Marta let herself be led forward, trying to ignore Ros's broad grin. "How's everything going?" Ros asked innocently.

"Fine," Marta said, signaling with a terse look not to say anything she'd have to explain to Evan. Luckily, a tall, muscular redhead sneaked behind Ros, tipped her wheelchair backwards and spun her around.

Ros screamed, then laughed as he pushed her down the sidewalk. "Make way!" he called out, and everyone cleared the path, like Moses parting the Red Sea.

"Abe! Would you stop that?" Ros's voice faded as the crowd closed in behind them.

"Her boyfriend?" Evan asked.

"He'd like to be," Marta explained. "Abe Sommers has been after her for years, but she insists that he doesn't need a cripple for a wife."

"I'm sure Abe doesn't see her as a cripple."

"No, but try getting it through Ros's head."

The owner of the hardware store and his wife fell into line behind them. While they talked to Evan, Marta's mind wandered back to Evan's failed romance.

Jill had either been a fool or extremely courageous to risk both her and her children's future on the strength of her ex-husband's promise. Her life could have become either heaven or hell. Luckily for her, Jill had got her happy ending.

People could change for the better, Marta supposed, but she wasn't brave enough to test the theory for herself.

By the time the sun had dropped below the tops of the trees, Marta felt more relaxed than she had since Evan had rolled into town. Ros had done the right thing by forcing her to bring Evan to the barbecue, although if Marta admitted it aloud, Ros wouldn't ever let her forget it.

The look of pleasure on his face as he dug into his

plate piled high with beef ribs and side dishes was immensely satisfying.

A while later she watched him as he lounged in a lawn chair, looking content with the world. "Did you get enough to eat?"

He groaned. "I shouldn't have taken that last brownie."

"It was a bit much," she agreed, "especially after you'd already gorged yourself on peanut-butter cookies, cherry pie and turtle cheesecake."

He patted his stomach. "I couldn't let the last piece of each go to waste. Besides, they looked so lonely by themselves."

She laughed. "They might have looked lonely, but their fat grams aren't. Think of all the calories you'll have to work off."

He grinned. "Yeah, but every bite was worth it."

Marta gazed over the crowd and saw Lynette Zindel slowly wind her way toward them. Her instincts kicked in—something was wrong.

Lynette approached with a smile on her face, but she spoke softly so no one could overhear. "I really hate to bother you," she apologized, "but Charlie is sick. Will you come?"

CHAPTER SIX

MARTA'S mind ran through all the possibilities, hoping the boy's immune system was strong enough to deal with whatever bug he might have caught.

"What's wrong?" she asked, aware of how quickly Evan sat at attention, his after-dinner lethargy instantly gone.

Lynette wrung her hands. "Charlie hardly ate any supper and now he's vomiting. Would you mind checking him, Dr Gallagher? It's probably nothing but..." she shrugged helplessly "...you know how over-protective moms are."

Evan rose. "Sure, I'll be happy to."

"He doesn't want people to worry, so would you play this low-key?"

He agreed. "Where is he?"

"In his room. First door on the right side of the hallway."

With that, Lynette turned away and ambled in the opposite direction.

Marta quickly swallowed her surprise at being ignored. The odd turn of events was rather unsettling. For a moment she felt like an abandoned toy, discarded because it had outlived its usefulness. Then she scolded herself for her thoughts. Why wouldn't the Zindels want a physician's opinion if they could get one? She couldn't afford to become territorial when her patients' lives were at stake.

After a circuitous route to the house, Marta followed Evan to Charlie's room. He knocked twice before a weak voice called out.

"Hey, there," Evan greeted the new teenager, who was lying on the twin-sized bed on his side. The room was pure boy, with a red-and-blue plaid bedspread and curtains to match. "I just heard horrible news. You're not enjoying all the good food."

The corners of Charlie's mouth turned up slightly. He held his stomach with one hand and clutched a hospital emesis basin with the other. "I don't know why she called you. I'm OK."

"Are you sure?" Evan asked. "I don't mind practicing my doctor stuff."

Once again a small grin tugged at Charlie's mouth. "OK," he agreed. "You won't find anything, though. I'm just tired, and when I'm tired I get nauseous."

Evan sat on the edge of the bed. "Do you have a thermometer handy?"

"Top drawer."

Where he'd indicated, Marta found the latest model in thermometers, along with tongue depressors, alcohol wipes and a penlight. She gave Evan the supplies he would use before she inserted the thermometer's tip into Charlie's ear. As soon as the signal beeped, she held it so Evan could read the digital display.

Ninety-nine point seven. Slightly elevated.

She took Charlie's pulse and counted his respirations. All normal.

"Did you get sick at camp?"

"I felt great."

"Did anyone get sick at camp? Colds, the flu, sore throat?"

Charlie thought a moment. "I heard one of the leaders got into poison ivy. Does that count?"

Evan smiled. "No."

"Then I don't think anyone was sick. The nurses watched us real close."

Evan probed the lymph glands in Charlie's neck, and checked his throat. "Can you roll onto your back for me?"

Charlie complied and Evan palpated his abdomen and pressed down on his right lower quadrant. "Does this hurt?"

"No."

Evan rose. "Looks like you were right, Charlie. I can't find a thing wrong with you."

"Told you so. Will you tell my mom, so she'll quit worrying?"

Marta laughed at his plaintive tone. "You bet. Are you going to be OK in here by yourself?"

"Yeah. I'm goin' to get ready for bed."

"Good idea," Evan said.

Charlie sat up. "Hey, thanks for the remote-control car, Marta. It's really cool."

She had spent hours agonizing over what a thirteen-year-old might want. She'd considered a CD, but wasn't sure of his taste in music. "I'm glad you enjoyed it. Sleep tight."

As they walked outside Lynette and her husband, Bob, met them at the door.

"His temp is up a little," Evan announced. "So far, though, no signs of infection."

Lynette's shoulders sagged and she let out a heavy sigh. "Thank goodness."

"If he's not better by morning, then call us."

"We will," Bob promised, shaking Evan's hand. "Thanks for the advice."

"My pleasure, but I really didn't do anything."

"You've given us peace of mind," Lynette declared. "It's worth a lot." Then, as if she'd remembered Marta's presence, she added, "Oh, but you've always been a big help to us, too, Marta. We don't want you to think—"

"I understand. You'd be foolish to settle for my opinion when you have an expert available." She smiled to ease Lynette's anxiety and to let Evan know she bore him no ill will. "Don't worry about it."

Lynette nodded. "Thanks again. To both of you."

Marta walked into the yard, conscious of Evan within arm's reach. Twilight was falling and someone had lit several yard candles to ward off the mosquitos. The crowd had thinned from its earlier standing-room-only capacity, but chairs were still at a premium.

She spied a wooden love seat under an oak tree several feet away from most of the group. While they were still close enough to carry on a conversation with the others if they spoke loudly, they could also talk privately between themselves.

"Nice night," she said once they'd sat down. Somehow the love seat had looked larger before they'd sat in it. Her leg rubbed against Evan's and she fought the urge to fidget. Instead, she clasped her hands together in her lap.

"Beautiful," he agreed. "The company makes it even better."

Marta wasn't about to fool herself into thinking he was referring specifically to *her* company. "New Hope is a friendly town," she said. "I've known these people for most of my life."

"Then you grew up here?"

She nodded. "After my mom left home, she married my dad and they lived in Blackwell, Oklahoma. He was killed right after I was born in a motorcycle accident. When I was five, my mom married Cooper Wyman and I suddenly had two younger sisters. We moved to New Hope when he was taken on at the feedlot."

"And you've stayed ever since."

"Yeah. Except for the years I went to college for my nursing and nurse-practitioner degrees."

"Did you always want to come home to work?"

She nodded. "Yes. A lot of people wouldn't go to the doctor until they were either deathly ill or it was too late. I wanted to make a difference."

"Sounds as if you did."

"Not as much as I'd like, though."

He rested his arm on top of the bench's back and the warmth from his skin tickled the nape of her neck. "If you could, what would you change?"

"You mean, other than having a doctor show up on a regular basis?" At his nod, she continued, "I'd like to have an X-ray machine. Nothing fancy, just something where I could snap a few pictures to check for pneumonia or broken bones. I know I couldn't cast them until I got more training, but at least I wouldn't have to send so many people to the ER with nothing more than a sprain.''

''That must be frustrating,'' he agreed.

''I'd also like a small instrument to check hemoglobins and white counts. Again, for a case like Charlie's, it would be nice to know right away if he's developed an infection and should be rushed to the hospital or not.''

''Have you talked to Campbell about this?''

''He says it's out of the question. Finances dictate what we can and can't do these days. We have to give the best patient care but at a fraction of the cost.'' She glanced at him. ''I'm not telling you anything you don't already know.''

''No,'' he said. ''However, my facility is fortunate because we can solicit donations to fill in the gaps.''

''Is that how you met my grandfather?''

Her final word seemed to hang in the evening air. ''I knew him long before I became a physician.''

''Really?'' Marta tried to imagine how a boy who had been forced to support his parents by working in a grocery store had crossed paths with the oil tycoon. Winston Clay most assuredly had a minion of servants who shopped for him.

''About six months after I found a job, your grandfather hired my mom as his cook and my dad as one of his grounds keepers. The cook's position came with a small apartment, so we moved in.

''When Winston came home at night, he'd always stop in the kitchen to see what was for dinner. I was usually doing homework, so he'd ask about my day. Later, after my dad died of a heart attack, Winston learned I wanted to go to med school and he helped me get there.''

She sensed she was getting the condensed version. In any case, it was obvious how highly Evan thought of Winston Clay. ''I see.''

''As you can tell, I carry a very different picture of him than you do.''

''He has only himself to blame,'' she said, hurt by the idea of Winston treating a stranger more like a grandchild than his own flesh and blood.

''Does he know you're here? In New Hope?'' she asked abruptly.

''Not yet, but he has my cellphone number, so I expect he'll call before long. He'll want to know if I'm enjoying his condo,'' he finished dryly.

Marta craned her neck to stare into his face. ''And what will you tell him?''

Although he hesitated, his gaze didn't waver. ''If he asks? The truth,'' he said simply.

''And what *is* the truth?''

Evan's mouth curled into a lazy grin. ''I'm enjoying a beautiful evening with his charming granddaughter.''

The intensity in his eyes, the husky quality to his tenor voice and the nearness of his body caused goose-bumps to rise on her bare skin and a shiver to zing its way down her spine.

Electricity seemed to charge the air. She focused her eyes on his mouth as her sense of smell honed in on his unique male scent mixed with the sweet tang of barbecue sauce.

In spite of being surrounded by people, nature provided the illusion of them being alone. The occasional call of a dove and the answering coo of its mate interrupted the song of the cicadas and the unrelenting chirp of an army of crickets.

"Tell me," he said softly, "would you ever consider leaving New Hope?"

Leave New Hope? His question cleared the fog surrounding her brain.

"I leave New Hope several times a month," she said, trying to read between the lines.

"To work," he corrected. "Would you ever consider working anywhere else?"

"Maybe." She shrugged. "If the conditions were right."

"And what constitutes the right conditions?"

She thought for a moment. "I'm not sure. Unlike most people, I'm satisfied with my salary and I enjoy my work at the clinic."

"What if the right person asked?"

She smiled. "If the right person asked, I'd definitely go, but only if I found a replacement. I may not be a physician, but I'm better than having no one at all.

"The people here are my friends," she added. "I won't desert them. Why do you want to know?"

"Just curious." Evan reached out to trace her mouth with his fingers and his eyes shone with a strange light. "I have the most remarkable urge to kiss you."

Just the thought that he *wanted* to kiss her sent Marta's spirits soaring. Remembering the man behind Evan's detour to New Hope, however, they quickly fell to earth.

"I'm afraid you'll have to restrain yourself."

He dropped his hand. "I know."

"I won't be bribed with a kiss."

"Bribed?"

"I won't change my mind about meeting my grandfather just because you kiss me," she explained primly.

For a long moment Evan appeared speechless. Suddenly he burst out laughing loud enough to attract attention.

"What's so funny?" she hissed.

"You are," he chortled. "You certainly are good for a man's ego."

"What's that supposed to mean?"

"I'm flattered. I never realized how powerful my kisses must be if they're capable of affecting your decisions."

"I wasn't paying you a compliment," she snapped, embarrassed because he found her remark humorous.

He hugged her. "I know."

His actual embrace proved what she'd always thought—the experience of being in his arms, however innocently, was too exhilarating for her to stay angry. She *had* sounded rather silly—prim, in fact. Marta burst out laughing.

Someone yelled out, "Hey, you two. What's so funny?"

"Sorry. Private joke," Evan returned as he released

her. He muttered for her ears only, "I don't know about you, but this place is too crowded."

His observation echoed her thoughts. "Where do you want to go?"

He shrugged. "You know this town better than I do. Besides, you're the driver. You decide."

"Have you seen the waterfall at the park?" she asked impulsively. She wasn't ready for the evening to end, but inviting him to her house was out of the question...not with her two sisters in town.

Relief flickered across his features. "Sounds great," he said with enthusiasm.

Their goodbyes lasted about half an hour and by then the sun had completely set. The lamps lining the city streets were already glowing brightly by the time they reached their destination.

Evan walked beside Marta on the concrete path winding through the city park, holding her loosely with one arm.

"You're walking too slowly if you want to burn off those extra calories," she teased.

He pulled her closer. "Don't you know you shouldn't exercise right after a big meal?"

"Your big meal was three hours ago."

He acted surprised. "My, how time flies. So, how many miles do we hike to find this waterfall?"

"It's around the bend. I'll warn you, though. Teenagers like to hang out here, too."

"Sort of like New Hope's Lovers' Lane?"

"Yeah." Perhaps it hadn't been such a good idea to bring him here.

Nonsense, she scolded herself. They were both

adults. Nothing…absolutely *nothing* would happen. She might toy with a few fantasies, but there were far too many reasons not to indulge in them.

"Tell me about Ros," he said as they passed under the leafy canopy the trees provided. "Has she always been in a wheelchair?"

"Oh, no. She rode horses and competed in shows all the time. One day she was practicing her jumps and for some reason her horse balked. She flew off, hit one of the fence's limestone posts and suffered a spinal-cord injury. Ever since then—she was thirteen at the time—she's been in a wheelchair."

"A severed spinal cord?"

"I'm not exactly sure," Marta admitted. "But whatever happened, the doctors gave her no hope."

"There's been a lot of progress made with those types of injuries. Has she gone back to see if they can repair the damage?"

Marta shook her head. "She's refused. I think she doesn't want to raise her hopes just to hear them give her the bad news all over again." She sighed. "I can't say I blame her."

The sound of water rushing grew louder. As she led him around the next curve, a small pool came into view. Illuminated by red, white and blue underwater lights, water shot through pipes of various lengths, creating fountains in a tiered design. At the north end of the pool, more water trickled down a steep eight-foot-tall and six-foot-wide brick staircase. Tiny strands of lights lined each step and created an illusion of millions of diamonds tumbling down.

"How unusual," he remarked.

She motioned to a lawn swing nearby, choosing the one shielded by several large bushes for added privacy. "It really is. Peaceful, too."

Minutes later, she was enjoying the gentle sway of the swing.

"How long has the clinic been in operation?" Evan asked.

"About two years. I finished nursing training when I was twenty-two. Afterwards, I worked in an ER while I studied to become a nurse-practitioner. Before I finished, I approached Dr Campbell about opening up a satellite clinic in New Hope. By the time I graduated, he'd agreed."

"He wasn't supportive of the idea?"

"Not at first. I had to work on him for several months. After I showed him facts and figures, and then spent two months working in his office to establish protocol and prove I could work independently, he was willing to try it."

"Did he furnish the building? It seems perfect for Ros and her wheelchair."

Marta smiled. "Oh, no. New Hope's city council provided the building, with the stipulation that Dr Campbell's clinic would sign a five-year contract. I'd always planned on hiring Ros, so I insisted on everything being wheelchair-accessible."

"You two must have been good friends."

"We *are* best friends," Marta corrected him. "While I was going to college, she was having a tough time because she'd planned on training horses and opening a riding academy. She was convinced her life was over, so I promised her a job. It gave her something to look forward to, so she took business and medical transcription classes at the community college. She did so well she received job offers from all over, but she turned them down. I'm lucky to have her.''

"Yes, you are. My own secretary could take a few lessons from her. Ros guards your time well."

Marta laughed. ''I've told her to relax, but she believes if we're lenient and give an inch, people will take the proverbial mile.''

"It happens a lot in service professions," he admitted. His voice grew soft. "Is that what happened when you went to Winston's office? His secretary wouldn't let you in?"

Marta stiffened and she fingered a fold of her dress. "I wish it had been that simple."

"What happened?"

It almost seemed like a dirty trick for Evan to mention a painful subject on such a pleasant evening, but the serenity of their surroundings gave her the courage to tell what she'd never told anyone else—not even Rachel. Marta had been too embarrassed for her stepsisters to learn that her own grandfather wouldn't give her the time of day when theirs was so kind.

She closed her eyes and inhaled the rich aroma of greenery and moss under the trees, the aroma of marigolds and zinnias, and the clean scent of water.

"My stepfather, Amy, Rachel and I had gone to Dallas after my mother died," she began. "We knew he'd leave the hotel for his appointment with some businessmen, so I planned to use the time to meet my grandfather and tell him of my mother's death. Rachel and I had worked everything out, including the cab fare, before we left home.

"My mom rarely talked about her dad and when she did she didn't say anything good about him. Understandable under the circumstances, but I was sure he'd want to know what had happened to her. So…" she drew a deep breath "…I took a taxi to his building and found him on the tenth floor. You can't imagine how scared I was to walk into his office."

"Yes, I can."

She hesitated. Sheer determination had kept her going after she'd seen Winston's name on the door in gold-plated letters. Perhaps if she'd made an appointment, their meeting wouldn't have been such a stressful experience. Then again, considering her rude reception, she probably wouldn't have been allowed into the elevator if she'd given advance notice of her arrival.

"I'd worn my newest dress, thinking it would boost my confidence," she admitted, recalling the short-sleeved, rose-print dress she'd sewn for the occasion. "I was petrified someone would throw me out before I could see him. At the same time, I had this overwhelming faith that once he knew who I was life would suddenly become wonderful. No more scraping by or doing without. A real Cinderella story."

Evan didn't answer, but she knew he understood.

"Anyway," she rushed on, "I walked into a room larger than our living room and kitchen combined. I asked the lady behind the desk—Ms Lancaster—if I could see Mr Clay because he was my grandfather.

"She gave me this funny look, then went into his

private office. When she came out, *he* was with her
and he was furious.'' Marta would never forget how
cold his expression had been. Icicles could have
dripped off his aristocratic nose.

"He instructed me to go back to wherever I'd come
from. He didn't have a granddaughter and my scam
wouldn't work.''

"Didn't you show him your birth certificate?''
Evan's voice was sharp, almost angry. She didn't
know if he was upset with her, or with Winston.

"I tried, but he wouldn't look at it because he
claimed it was falsified. Then he threatened to call the
police.''

"I'm so sorry,'' Evan murmured.

If he hadn't sympathized, she would have remained
in control. The pity on his face was her undoing.

Marta's eyes glistened and she sniffled. "I wanted
him to believe me so much,'' she whispered, reliving
the moment, "and he thought I was lying.''

Nothing had crushed her tender heart as thoroughly
as his accusation. After thirteen years, she could still
hear his voice thundering in her ears, taste the fear in
her mouth.

She hiccuped and pressed her lips together as she
struggled to regain her composure. Without a word,
Evan tugged her close and tucked her head under his
chin. As he whispered nothings to her and stroked her
back, her emotions burst through the walls she'd
erected around herself.

"I hate to cry,'' she said through her tears.

"I know.''

"I told myself after that day, I never would cry again over him."

Evan was sure she hadn't. Until now. Although he hated to be the one who brought her to this point, releasing her hurt was long overdue.

"Why wouldn't he know who I was?" Marta asked in a choked voice. "Couldn't he see enough of his own child in me to at least ask a few questions?"

Torn between his sorrow for her and his loyalty to Winston, he didn't know what to say. All he could do was hold her...and soothe away her anguish as best he could.

Her quiet sobs continued as if now that the dam had broken loose the water wouldn't stop until every last drop of grief over her disappointments, rejections and lost dreams had been expelled.

His shirt became sodden, but he didn't care. He wanted her to lean against him and draw from his strength while she had none left of her own.

Finally, she sniffled, and he knew the well was running dry. Yet she continued to cling to him and he was more than happy to keep her nestled against his chest.

"The lady walked me to the elevator," she said softly. "Isn't it odd how I remember what she was wearing? A navy-blue suit with a striped blue-and-white silk scarf around her neck. And I remember her perfume. Something sophisticated."

"It was an intense time for you." People's brains often recorded the most minute details during a crisis.

"Yeah. Everything seemed to happen in slow motion. Anyway, she escorted me to the elevator.

Probably to make sure I didn't hang around and cause trouble," she said wryly. "I asked if I could leave my address in case he changed his mind. She was nice about it, and smiled, but said not to bother. Nothing would come of it."

"I wish you hadn't had to go through that," he said.

Marta straightened, wiping her tear-streaked face with her fingertips. Evan reluctantly let her go.

"Do you understand why I find it difficult to believe in his sincerity? Or does he finally want to see me because I made my own way and he won't have to spend any of his millions on my behalf?"

"Don't be ridiculous," he said firmly. "Can't you give him the benefit of the doubt? Talk to him for yourself and let him answer your questions."

He felt her gaze search his face in the semi-darkness. "I know you want me to, but I can't. Please, try to understand. I want to forget I ever met him. I want to forget that Winston Clay is my grandfather."

Evan fell silent. For several long minutes the splashing water provided the only background noise as he considered his reply.

"I know you want to pretend he doesn't exist," he finally said. "But you never have and you never will."

"Of course I have," she retorted. "I was fine until you came."

He shook his head. "You may think you were, but consider what you've done with your life. Everything you've accomplished was intended to prove one thing.''

"Which is?''

"That you didn't need him.''

"I didn't,'' she said coolly. "I still don't.''

He shrugged. "Perhaps. However, your determination to become a success without his help was what drove you. It still does, if you'd only admit it. So, do you honestly believe you'll ever forget him?''

She squared her shoulders and met his gaze without flinching. "I'm going to try.''

CHAPTER SEVEN

EVAN'S cellphone rang on Saturday morning and he pried open his eyes to check the time. Nine a.m. An ungodly hour, considering he'd fallen asleep just before dawn. After Marta had given him a ride back to the motel, he'd been too keyed up to go to bed. The combination of her tragic story and his unfulfilled desire for her had kept the sandman away.

In the end, he'd watched television and tried to read the latest Robin Cook mystery, before giving up at five a.m.

Now, with the melodic twitter in his ear, he shook himself awake.

"Evan," a hearty voice announced. "How are you?"

He mentally groaned. He'd promised to touch bases with Winston and his mother after he'd settled in. After two weeks and no word, they'd obviously grown concerned.

"I'm fine, Winston," he said, rubbing the sleep out of his eyes. "Just relaxing and enjoying myself." He *had* enjoyed himself last night, so he wasn't lying.

"The weather channel shows it's perfect there in the mountains."

"It is. Warm days and cool nights." Evan repeated what he knew to be true before he steered the subject in another direction. He didn't want to bluff his way through another conversation about local conditions. "How's Mom?"

"She's right here." Before Evan knew it, his mother had the phone.

"Are you looking after yourself?" she asked. "Getting plenty of rest and eating right?"

"I'm fine, Mom." Ruth Gallagher conveniently forgot how at thirty-three years old he didn't need her to monitor his daily diet.

"We expected you to call before now."

Her gentle chiding sent a twinge of remorse through him. "I'm sorry. It's just been…busy." He winced at his description.

"You're there to rest, not to be busy, dear. Take care, son. Winston wants to talk again."

He heard the phone jiggling before Winston's voice came across the miles. "I hated to call you on your cellphone, but I never could reach you at the condo."

"I'm not inside very often."

"I see." The pause was brief. "I was hoping you'd tell me how you liked the exercise equipment I had installed."

"I haven't tested everything out yet," he said, hating to stretch the truth, "but it all looks great. I'll give it a whirl on the next rainy day."

"Evan?"

Something in Winston's tone changed, and Evan grew wary. "Yes?"

"There isn't any exercise equipment in the condo."

Damn! "Oh."

"Where *are* you?"

Evan sighed as he pinched the bridge of his nose. So much for keeping his whereabouts a secret. "New Hope."

"Dear boy! Have you been there the entire time?"

"I'm afraid so."

"Then you've seen Marta." It wasn't a question and Evan could hear the excitement in Winston's voice.

"Yes. She's a lovely young lady."

"Well?" Winston demanded. "I need details."

Evan tried to assemble an explanation that wouldn't devastate the older man. At seventy-five, he didn't need unnecessary stress, even if he still oversaw all of his company holdings.

"I'm working with her on a temporary basis."

"Working? You're supposed to be on vacation. Recuperating."

"I know. I am. Honest."

"Has she mentioned me at all?"

If anyone else had asked him that question, Evan would have replied without hesitation. *She hates your guts and, oh, by the way, I'd like to go a few rounds with you for what you did to her.*

However, because Winston had asked the question, and because Evan was committed to helping him right past wrongs, he offered a more neutral response.

"We've talked about you, yes."

"And?"

"We've reached the stage where I can mention your name and she won't throw me out of the room."

"That bad?"

"Oh, not quite." Close, he thought. Yet how could

he say more? It would crush Winston to know how he'd single-handedly alienated his only granddaughter. "But I'm making progress."

"I don't blame her for being upset with me. She came to my office when she was about fifteen, didn't she?"

Evan wanted to disagree, and couldn't, especially since Winston sounded as if he'd known it all along. "Yes, she did."

Winston sounded tired. Defeated. "I thought so."

"She told me the story," Evan said, cautiously. "What happened?"

"I don't know where to begin." Winston sighed. "About a week before Marta arrived in my office, one of the tabloids had unearthed information about my daughter, Lily. They ran a story full of half-truths and the next thing I knew I had people coming out of the woodwork, claiming to be my lost granddaughter. They all carried proof of some sort. One girl even tried to pass off a piece of fabric that supposedly came from one of Lily's dresses."

"It must have been hard."

"You can't imagine," Winston said wryly. "You see, years earlier I'd been told of Lily being killed in a car accident, along with her husband and newborn child. Those facts had been verified, so I sent everyone who claimed to be my grandchild away without a hearing."

Evan could guess at the number of unscrupulous people who'd tried to capitalize on the story.

"Unfortunately, Marta was caught in the backlash. When my secretary informed me of yet another teenager who claimed she was a relative, I stormed out of my office ready to unleash the wrath of God. I've made grown men shiver in their socks on occasion, but not this little girl. She stood there and didn't say a word.'' His voice sounded as if he were revisiting the scene in his mind.

''Then…'' he paused ''…she calmly thanked me for my time, and left.''

Evan could easily imagine a young Marta squaring her shoulders, raising her chin and staring defiantly at the man who'd taken away her hopes and dreams.

Winston cleared his throat. ''The incident stayed with me for years. When I received the newspaper article a few months ago, I hired another investigator. To my surprise, he discovered that my daughter *hadn't* been killed in a car accident. If the man I'd originally employed hadn't died in the interim, I would have ruined him.''

Winston didn't issue idle threats, and he was upset enough to follow through.

''Of course, this confirmed what Marta had told me.'' His voice grew husky. ''My granddaughter had actually come to me and I'd turned her away. To my utter regret, I had no way of finding her.''

''Don't lose hope yet,'' Evan said, hating to hear the defeat in Winston's tone. ''Give me time. She'll come around.'' It didn't hurt to remain optimistic.

''I don't know. She may not ever forgive me.''

'''It's not over till it's over,''' Evan quoted.

''I realize she won't talk to me, so would you pass along a message? Tell her how sorry I am?''

''I will.''

"Good." Winston's voice grew stronger. "How is life in New Hope? If I recall, it isn't a booming town."

"No, it's not, which is OK because it gives me time to myself."

"Have you reached any decisions about your career yet?"

"No decisions, but I haven't missed the dinner parties where my job was to collect bank drafts."

Then again, he knew the importance of those donations to people like Charlie Zindel. Was he being selfish to look after his wants rather than doing what would benefit the most people?

"The answer will come in due time," Winston predicted. "You'll know when you know which way to go."

Evan grinned. "I'm counting on it."

"You'll keep me posted on the situation with Marta?"

"Wild horses couldn't stop me." He might have to edit his report, but he'd pass along news of his progress.

"Oh, and, Evan?" Winston asked. "I appreciate what you did—trying to protect my feelings."

Evan smiled. "You've always been too smart for your own good."

"However," Winston said sternly, "if you ever do it again, I'll have your mother ground you for a month of Sundays."

Evan laughed at the familiar but empty threat. "You always did know how to keep me in line."

Winston chuckled. "Just don't forget it."

As he snapped the phone closed, Evan realized how Winston had always treated him and his parents as part of the family rather than as employees. Clearly the Gallaghers had filled the void Winston experienced in his life while Marta had allowed the people of New Hope to fill hers.

If only he could get Marta to enjoy the same easy-going relationship with her grandfather that he did. He wanted it not just for Winston's happiness but because Marta was becoming more important to him than he'd ever expected or imagined possible.

He admired her for her strength in adversity, for her loyalty toward the people in New Hope and for her genuine concern for those in her charge. Her generosity of spirit went bone-deep, which was why he believed her attitude toward her grandfather could be softened.

It *had* to change. Otherwise, he'd be forced to choose between the two people who meant as much to him as his own parents.

He only had one option. He had to pull Marta back into the circle where she belonged.

Oddly enough, Marta felt as if unburdening herself had taken a huge weight off her shoulders. At least Evan now understood and would respect her wishes. She'd taken enough psychology classes to know, however, that at some point in the future those shadows in her past would have to be confronted and the ghosts exorcised.

In the meantime, she'd live for the moment and enjoy each day as it came.

"You're mighty chipper this morning," Ros said as Marta sailed through the door on Monday. "Must have been a great weekend."

"It certainly wasn't boring," Marta admitted, thinking of her evening with Evan and her gab session with her sisters.

"Now aren't you glad I arranged for you to give Dr Gallagher a ride?"

"Will it go to your head if I agree?"

Ros grinned. "Probably, but do it anyway."

"We had a very nice time."

"'Nice' sounds so…insipid," Ros said. "Can't you think of any better adjectives? Like wonderful, stupendous or the-best-night-of-my-life?"

"Let's not get carried away," Marta protested. "I had a nice time. Period." Those hours spent at the park had become infinitely precious and she wasn't ready to share them with anyone, not even her best friend.

Ros motioned toward Marta's burden. "Speaking of being carried, what's in the basket?"

"I made my Mexican casserole yesterday, so I thought Evan might help me with the leftovers. You're welcome to join us."

"Sorry. Two's company and three's a crowd."

"No, really. I have plenty."

Ros shook her head. "I can't. Other plans. Abe's taking me out."

"You finally agreed to go?"

Ros shrugged. "He's bugged me for so long, I felt sorry for him. Don't read anything into it."

"If you won't read anything into me sharing a home-cooked meal with Evan."

"It's a deal. Did your sisters stay for the weekend?"

"Yeah. They left yesterday." Marta changed the subject. "What's on the schedule for today?"

"From the looks of things, I hope you'll have time to enjoy your casserole," Ros said. "You're booked solid."

Considering she handled a lot of screening procedures, physical exams and check-ups to monitor medication, she usually was busy. "Evan, too?"

"He won't be twiddling his thumbs," Ros declared.

"Then we'd better get started. Is he here?"

"In the office." Ros glanced at the clock. "You have about ten minutes before your first patient."

Marta placed the food in the kitchenette's refrigerator and headed down the corridor, feeling somewhat uneasy but also eager to see Evan. He hadn't wanted to leave her alone after she'd unburdened herself, and he'd reluctantly agreed to do so after she'd reminded him of her sisters being in town. Had they been gone, she wouldn't have hesitated to accept his offer.

Thinking of how many times she'd reassured him, of how many times he'd encouraged her to call regardless of the hour, she smiled. Being the strong one in the family, the one who kept things together by sheer will and looked after the others, it was nice to be on the receiving end of someone's concern.

She stood on the threshold, hating to break his obvious concentration. Instead, she took the opportunity to look her fill. He wore clothes she'd seen before, but somehow he seemed different. Probably because today she saw him through different eyes.

A small lock of hair hung down on his forehead as he pored over the page in his hand. His eyebrows were furrowed and he appeared deep in thought.

Staring at his full lips, she wished he'd kissed her last night. Just thinking about pressing her mouth to his, feeling his skin touch hers and having his unique scent surround her, it sent an anticipatory quiver down her spine.

Evan raised his head and a slow smile slid across his features. "Hi. How are you?"

Marta knew he wasn't asking about her physical health. "I'm fine," she said, entering with a smile. "Getting an early start?"

"Yeah. I'm trying to figure out why Mrs Lopez continues to exhibit signs of hypertension. All of her urinary tests came back within normal limits."

"So what's next? Medication?"

He frowned. "I hate to resort to medication at her age, but we've ruled out everything else. I wonder now if we missed something. She's not taking any other medicine, is she?"

"None that I've prescribed."

He shrugged. "Maybe something will jump out at me during her appointment."

"Let's hope so."

Before Marta could ask about his other patients, she heard the familiar buzzer. "There's our signal," she said. "I'll see who's here. Oh, before I forget, I brought lunch, if you'd care to join me."

His grin sent her stomach into a flip-flop. "It's a date."

Marta greeted Monica with mild weariness and ushered her into the closest room.

"I just can't catch my breath," Monica rasped. "And I feel like I'm choking. You have to do something."

"I'll do my best." She quickly took care of the basics, then listened carefully to the woman's chest.

No rattles, no wheezes, nothing. This was one time when Marta wished for an X-ray unit. She slung her stethoscope around her neck. "Your temp is normal, your pulse is a little fast, but your lungs sound clear."

"Really?" Monica appeared surprised. "But I can't breathe and can hardly swallow."

"What did you eat last?"

"My usual bowl of bran flakes and strawberries."

Marta jumped on a possibility. "Are you allergic to strawberries or other foods?"

"Not at all," Monica declared. "I don't even have hay fever."

Marta was truly stymied and needed a second opinion. Thank goodness she had a physician on site for situations like this. "I'm going to ask Dr Gallagher to see you."

Monica frowned. "I won't have to pay extra, will I?"

Marta hid a smile. "No."

"Then I suppose it's OK."

Marta slipped from the room with her notes. "I've

got a case for you," she said as soon as she entered their office. "Monica Taylor."

He leaned back in the chair. "The lady who comes in every week?" At Marta's nod, he asked, "What's her story today?"

"She says she can't breathe and has difficulty in swallowing. Her temp is normal, along with everything else. Her lungs sound clear. I thought it might be allergy-related, but she says she's never reacted to anything before."

"What about asthma?"

"Not so far. Would you mind…?"

He rose, and she added, "Don't forget your sunglasses."

"Sunglasses?"

"She's wearing hot pink and fluorescent green."

He grinned. "Thanks for the warning." Inside Monica's room, he introduced himself and began what Marta considered a thorough exam.

"I'm really enjoying my stay in New Hope," he mentioned casually to his patient. "It seems like such a nice place to raise a family. Did you raise yours here?"

"Yes. The mister and I had three children. Two girls and a boy."

"Are they still in town?"

"Oh, no. They've all moved away."

"Any grandchildren?"

"Two. My oldest girl had twin boys. They live in Colorado Springs."

Marta watched Evan painstakingly take Monica's pulse, recheck her temperature, look in her ears, nose and throat, and listen to her chest. Maybe he would find something she'd overlooked.

He smiled and continued without missing a beat of their conversation. "What about your other two children?"

"The middle girl lives in Garden City, and my son is in Wichita."

"They're not too far away, then," he said. "I'll bet they come home often."

"No, they don't."

"People are busy these days," he said. "It's hard to take a trip, especially if the children are involved in a lot of activities."

"Bobbi and Reed don't have kids. They don't come home unless they need money. I told them not to bother if that was all they wanted me for."

Marta suddenly formed a suspicion about Monica's mysterious illnesses. Evan's eyes gleamed with a similar awareness.

"Maybe if you invited them for a visit," Marta suggested. "For your birthday or another special occasion."

"We'll see." She peered at Evan. "So, why can't I breathe?"

Evan glanced at Marta. "Do we have a PulmoAide?"

"Yes," she said slowly, understanding his request but not the reason for it.

"Good. Mrs Taylor, I want to try something. Marta will prepare a solution of medicine for you to inhale—a breathing treatment like you'd get at the hospital. After twenty minutes, let's see how you're feeling."

"Thank you, Doctor."

Marta followed Evan out of the room. "What do you mean by giving her an inhalation treatment? There's nothing wrong with her!"

"You and I both know it, but she doesn't."

"We can't treat her for a non-existent condition."

"I'm not treating her. I'm conducting a test. I think she's experiencing a panic attack. Fill the nebulizer with normal saline. If she can breathe easier by the time she's finished, her problem is psychological."

"It's worth a try," she said. "What made you think of mentioning her family?"

"I couldn't find a physical problem. After what Mrs Taylor said, I think she wants us to find something seriously wrong with her so her children will come home. She's probably trying to see where their loyalties are—with her or her bank account. All of which explains why she presents with a new symptom every week. If I'm right, I'll encourage her to seek counseling."

"Wouldn't it be easier to contact her daughter?"

"Yes, but we can't," Evan said. "Mrs Taylor is mentally competent to care for herself. If we discuss her medical condition with her family without her permission, we're asking for a lawsuit."

Marta shook her head in amazement. "OK. You're the doctor. I just hope your diagnosis is right."

He grinned. "Me, too."

As he'd predicted, twenty minutes later Monica was all smiles. "What was wrong with me?" she asked Evan. "Can I get one of those machines at home?"

"I'm afraid your breathing problem was more emotional than physical," he said kindly. "Don't feel bad. A lot of people suffer panic attacks when they're under stress."

"Emotional? Panic attack?" Monica grew angry. "I'm not going crazy!"

"I didn't say you were," Evan said. "Sometimes people get burdened down with their thoughts, and as a result they experience symptoms like those you've described. I'd recommend professional counseling."

"Counseling? Could I see someone here in town?"

Marta interrupted. "The agency nearest us is in Liberal."

Monica frowned. "Too far." Her face brightened. "I know. I'll talk to my minister. He's got all these fancy initials after his name."

"Good idea," Evan said before he sent Monica on her way.

"Do you honestly think her minister will help her?" asked Marta.

"Who knows? She needs to talk to someone, and if the choice is a man of the cloth or no one at all, I'll take my chances."

"I guess you're right. I wonder if she'll be back next week?" Marta asked.

"It's hard to say. Until she deals with her family problems, she'll continue having symptoms. The question is, will she see you or her pastor?"

"I'd better bone up on my psychiatric nursing."

He grinned. "You guessed it."

After several other minor cases, Juanita Lopez was next in line. Marta escorted her into the room while Evan explained her test results.

"Everything we've done has been normal," he told her.

Juanita stared up at him as she sat on the exam table. "This is good news, no?"

"Yes, it is. Unfortunately, I still don't know what's causing your high blood pressure," he admitted. "Are you taking any other medication?"

"Pills?" she asked.

"Yes."

Juanita slowly shook her head. "No. No pills."

"What about over-the-counter medicine?" Marta thought of all the products on the drug-store shelves. Vitamins, minerals, herbs. "Are you taking any herbal supplements?"

Juanita's face brightened. "Herbs. *Si*. Rosemary."

"Rosemary?" Marta turned to Evan. "Does it have any side-effects?"

He gave her a tight smile. "Oh, yes."

"I have not had any problems," Juanita boasted. "The rosemary, it is *wonderful*. My cousin, she tells me how two cups of rosemary tea a day helps the hair to grow and stop falling out so I use it for this. I also put the oil in the bath to help stiff muscles after working in the garden."

"Were you drinking just two cups a day?" Evan asked.

Juanita giggled. "I drink three, sometimes four. I want lots of healthy hair. The women in my family don't have thick hair."

Marta studied Juanita's head. If the rosemary tea had made a difference, she couldn't see it.

"Rosemary is used to improve the circulation," Evan explained, "which in turn can affect the blood pressure. You're drinking more than the recommended dose, plus bathing in it every night, so you might be overdosing yourself."

Juanita's expression turned to one of horror. "Oh, my goodness. If two cups are good, then four should be better, no?"

"No," Evan said. "Don't drink any more tea."

"No more rosemary? Not even in my bath?"

"No. At least not for a while," Evan conceded. "I want Marta to check your blood pressure in about three weeks. If it's gone down, we've found the culprit."

Juanita's disappointment was palpable. "No rosemary for three weeks. *Si*. I understand."

After Juanita had left, Marta shook her head. "I never considered a herb when I asked her what she was taking."

"Apparently she didn't consider her tea as medicinal either. If she's lucky, eliminating the rosemary should bring her BP down and we'll have solved another mystery."

Marta laughed. "I'll keep my fingers crossed."

Evan glanced at the wall clock. "It's almost noon and I'm starved. I hope you brought plenty."

At that second, Ros braked to a stop in front of them. "Better forget about lunch."

A sense of foreboding came over her as Ros went

on, "There's been an accident. Frank requested you two to come."

"Isn't he the paramedic?" Evan asked.

"Yes," Marta answered. "What happened?"

"Some sort of construction accident near the south end of town," Ros reported. "The highway crew has been replacing the drainage culvert. Someone is trapped underneath."

CHAPTER EIGHT

MARTA ran to the supply cupboard, pulled out a trauma pack she kept on hand and tossed it to Evan, before she yanked another tackle box off the shelf.

"Let's go. We'll take my Jeep."

In a few seconds flat Marta was heading toward the location of the accident with Evan beside her.

"Do you always bring extra supplies?" he asked, hanging onto the roll bar as she turned a corner on two wheels.

"Usually. We don't normally need them, but I'd rather have extra than not enough."

Marta sailed through town, aware of Evan's white-knuckled grip but impressed by his stoicism. "We'll be there in another minute or so," she said.

The stoplight ahead had turned yellow, but she gunned the engine to zoom through the intersection before the color switched to red.

"Done any stock-car racing?" he asked.

"Don't worry. I'll get us there in one piece."

If he replied, the wind carried it out of earshot.

Flashing lights of a police cruiser blocked off the road. Marta slowed to a crawl, but the officer waved her on ahead where every emergency vehicle owned by the city of New Hope was parked. City and county highway employees stood helplessly in a group, their faces black with dirt and covered with worry. She pulled up next to the ambulance and hopped out while Evan followed.

As they hurried toward the stretch of road where the viaduct was being replaced, she saw a large concrete drainage cylinder lying haphazardly to one side of the road. An arm appeared outstretched from underneath it and a host of emergency personnel had closed ranks around the victim.

Marta forced her mind to think of the task at hand rather than the individual involved.

To her relief, Evan took charge. "Coming through," he called.

The men parted, allowing them access. "How much time have we lost?" he asked.

Marta stared at the victim lying on the ground with only his head, shoulders and one arm exposed. Blood trickled from his mouth although he didn't appear conscious. One EMT knelt near his head and monitored the oxygen flow through the non-rebreather mask. Marta tossed Evan a pair of latex gloves, before donning her own, and Frank spoke as he tried to start an IV.

"It happened about ten minutes ago. They were lifting the culvert off the truck when the chain broke. It dropped several feet, hitting the truck and rolling off the bed. Everyone managed to jump out of the way, except for Chico."

"Vitals?"

Frank recited a low blood pressure and a rapid heart rate. "Distended jugular."

"Stethoscope," Evan ordered. Marta pulled hers out of her pocket and handed it to him. He slid against the edge of the huge drainage pipe and tucked the chestpiece against the part of Chico's chest he could reach.

For a long time he didn't say a word. Finally, he straightened and gave his report. "Heart sounds are muffled."

The significance didn't escape Marta, and as she exchanged a quick glance with Frank she read the same, unmistakable message in his eyes.

The three observations—decreased blood pressure, distended jugular veins and muffled heart sounds—formed what was called Beck's triad. The results they'd noted were all typical of pericardial tamponade, where an injury to the heart caused the blood to flow into the pericardial sac surrounding the organ.

If they could remove the concrete in time to stop the bleeding… If they could even halt the bleeding… If they could reverse the pressure caused by the blood accumulating around the heart…and if his heart and lungs weren't crushed beyond their capacity to function, Chico might live.

Those were a lot of ifs to pin any hopes on.

Evan turned to the fire chief who was overseeing both the emergency and the highway department crews as they worked frantically to ready the concrete for lifting. "What's taking so long?" he demanded.

"Had to find another chain. Just a few more minutes, Doc."

Evan glanced at Marta. She would have missed the imperceptible shake of his head if she hadn't been watching him so carefully.

"Keep the O_2 going," he instructed.

Frank hesitated, before he acknowledged the order. True to his training, he continued to monitor Chico's blood pressure as best as he could.

The fire chief crouched beside the group. "We're ready if you are."

Adrenalin surged through Marta and she steeled herself for what they would see.

"OK, guys," Evan told them. "As soon as he's out, we'll do what we can."

Marta nodded and poised herself to spring into action. "Got it."

Evan motioned to another fireman hovering nearby. "You and Frank will drag him out on my command. I'll tell you when there's enough clearance. Wait for my signal. Marta? Move back."

With grim determination etched on their faces, both men fastened their attention on Evan and prepared to grab Chico's shoulders.

Evan lay back on the ground, wiggling against the unyielding concrete. Marta reluctantly obeyed his instruction to stand out of harm's way, but remained close enough to step in when the time came. Waiting was terrible, and her silent prayer was for the three men who, if this chain broke, could be crushed like insignificant bugs.

A minute later he called out, "Ready."

The chief passed along the word, raising his hand at the same time. "Let's go. Easy now."

Unable to take her gaze off the scene, Marta heard the gears grinding as the crane operator slowly shifted his levers. The slack in the chain slowly disappeared until at last the links grew taut.

With a shudder and a small bounce, the metal groaned. Slowly, the concrete lifted in small increments while a group of men steadied it with their hands. Marta didn't breathe in case the slightest extraneous motion brought about more disaster.

"Now!" Evan yelled. At the same time he rolled away from the cylinder and bounded to his feet. Instantly, Chico was pulled free and moved to a safer distance.

Evan grabbed Chico's shirt and ripped, exposing the man's sunken and purple-colored chest.

Marta knelt beside the man she knew to be in his mid-twenties, objectively cataloguing the rest of his injuries from his neck to his pelvis. Intent on doing her job, she hardly noticed the rumble of the earth beneath her as the concrete settled back on the ground under the guiding influence of many pairs of hands.

"I'm losing him," Frank shouted, although raising his voice wasn't necessary since they were all kneeling around the young man. "No BP."

Evan's hands pressed on Chico's chest as he assessed the damage. It seemed to take for ever but actually only took a few seconds. It was clear to everyone that no amount of intervention would be enough.

Evan sat back on his heels. "Every rib feels broken. Chances are the impact ruptured his aorta and crushed everything inside. Poor guy didn't have a chance."

Marta had suspected as much, but the knowledge didn't diminish her grief over the loss of this young man's life.

"What's the time?" he asked calmly.

Frank glanced at his watch. "Twelve-fifteen."

"Time of death, twelve fifteen," Evan pronounced as he rose.

With grim faces, Frank and his fellow EMTs removed the IVs and the oxygen mask. He motioned with his head toward his truck, and a few minutes later someone came running with a black body bag.

Marta busied herself by gathering the litter strewn over the ground. Sometimes performing the most mundane of tasks helped hold the pain to manageable levels.

To her surprise, Evan assisted Frank and the other EMTs with the body. He didn't have to help; it wasn't expected. In fact, it was most unusual for a physician to perform such a humbling act.

Then again, Evan Gallagher was a most unusual man.

His respectful handling of a person he'd never seen before brought a lump to Marta's throat. Now wasn't the time to realize she would miss him horribly when he left. It wasn't the time to realize that no one she'd ever met, or ever *would* meet, could compare. Nor was it the time to realize how badly she wanted to spend her life learning everything about him.

She watched him load the body into the ambulance, strip off his gloves, then approach the local authorities who stood within hearing distance.

"You'll notify the next of kin?" Evan asked.

Nate Brooks, the rotund police chief of a four-officer force, nodded. "We'll take care of things."

"There wasn't anything we could do," Evan added.

"No one thought you could, Doc. Don't worry, I'll make sure the family understands."

"You'll notify the coroner?"

Nate nodded at Evan's question. "We'll drive the body to the morgue in Liberal. Dr Edwards will do the autopsy."

Any fatal on-the-job accident required a post-mortem exam for legal purposes. The pathologist would determine the exact cause of death and either rule out or implicate drug abuse.

For the sake of Chico's family, Marta hoped the drug tests were negative, although she didn't have reason to assume otherwise. Chico was as straight as an arrow and everyone in town knew it. However, insurance companies looked for ways to avoid paying death benefits, and employers protected themselves against negligence lawsuits if they could prove a person had been under the influence at the time of an accident.

Marta finished her self-appointed task. As she tossed the last wrapper into a trash bag, Frank took it from her and knotted it.

"Thanks for coming, Marta," the paramedic said. "When I got here, I didn't think he was alive. Even though he was, well...I never figured he'd make it to the hospital. There are times when a man hopes he's wrong."

"I'm glad you asked for us," she said.

Frank motioned toward Evan. "I'm glad he was here."

"Me, too, Frank. Me, too."

Without a word, she gathered her unneeded supplies and headed for her Wrangler. She didn't want to see the faces of the curiosity-seekers now lining the police barricade or the horrified expressions of Chico Rodriguez's co-workers, so she kept her head down. Idly, she noticed her uniform was liberally covered with dirt from kneeling on the ground. Evan fell into step beside her. "Let me take that," he said, removing the bulky trauma kit from her fingers before she could protest.

After dropping the carry-all into the back seat, he held out his hand. Wordlessly, she handed him the car keys. She was fully capable of driving, but knew Evan would prefer to sit behind the wheel himself.

He turned the ignition key. "Where to?" he asked. "The office?"

Marta shook her head. "I need to change clothes before I see any patients."

"Yeah. I'd better do the same."

"Why don't you drop me at my place, then come back after you're ready?" she suggested, before she recited her address.

"Do you trust me with your Jeep?" he asked.

She'd already given him her heart, so placing her vehicle in his care seemed rather inconsequential. However, she couldn't express her thoughts so she hid her true feelings behind a joke.

"Are there dark secrets in your driving past?" she teased. "Things like grand theft larceny?"

He laughed. "Only a speeding ticket when I was eighteen."

"Speeding?" She pretended to be horrified.

"Believe me," he assured her, "I wasn't going as fast as you were earlier. I'm surprised the FAA didn't cite us for not filing a flight plan."

"It wasn't that bad," she protested.

"I don't know," he said, shaking his head slowly from side to side. "You weren't hanging on for dear life."

For the space of a few seconds the day had seemed normal. Those few words brought the tragedy flooding back in living color. Her smile dimmed.

"I'm sorry," he said, reaching for her hand.

"It's OK," she said. "We'd better go. Ros will be wondering if we're playing hookey."

"We could, you know," he said as he drove away from the tragic scene.

The idea held a certain appeal, but if she gave in to her impulse, it could easily become a habit.

"Yeah, but it's better if I stay busy. Less time to think."

"You're right."

Evan drove her home. Aware of her uncommunicative mood, he didn't try to force a conversation. Everyone handled situations such as this differently. Some people clammed up while others simply chattered non-stop in an effort to push it out of their minds.

"He was twenty-four," Marta commented idly.

Instinctively, Evan knew she was referring to their victim. Talking was a good catharsis for the soul, and so he listened.

"Did you know he was going to get married next

month? That's why his dad, Joe, came in and had the lipoma excised. So he'd look nice for the pictures.''

Evan made the mental connection. Sadly, those photos would never be taken, but he didn't state the obvious.

''Chico delivered newspapers when he was a kid,'' she said idly. ''He had quite an aim. He was one of the few who could hit our front porch.''

''Quite a feat,'' he said, pulling to a stop in front of her house. It was a white frame house with a small porch, and resembled every other one on the block. The only difference lay in the trim. Marta's shutters had a border of hearts cut into the wood and were painted a robin's-egg blue.

Marta stared into the distance, making no effort to leave the vehicle. ''Life can be the pits.''

''At times,'' he agreed. ''Which is why we have to make the most of our days. We never know what tomorrow will bring.''

Her hazel eyes met his. ''Is this where you remind me to mend fences with my grandfather?''

Evan gave her a half-smile. ''You reminded yourself.''

''I'm not ready,'' she said flatly. ''I don't know if I ever will be.''

Evan wondered if he might do irrevocable harm by discussing this—but nothing ventured, nothing gained. ''I spoke him with on Sunday,'' he began slowly. ''I learned something interesting.''

She didn't cover her ears, so he pressed on. ''At the time you came to his office, a tabloid had run the story of Winston and his daughter, Lily, conveniently leaving out the details of her death. Consequently, people came out of the woodwork, all claiming to be his grandchild. He didn't believe any of them, including you, because he thought you'd both died years earlier.''

"If you're trying to get me to feel sorry for him—''

"I'm only relating the facts so you'll understand why Winston reacted the way he did,'' he interrupted. "He asked if I'd tell you he's sorry. For everything.''

Marta nibbled on her bottom lip and stared through the windshield.

"If he could possibly undo that day, he would,'' he added. "Will you give him a second chance?''

Marta slid out of the passenger's seat and slammed the door before she met his gaze. "I'll think about it.''

She didn't refuse him outright, so he took it as a good sign. "Shall I come back in, say, thirty minutes to an hour?''

"Fine. I'll leave the door unlocked.''

After she went inside, he headed for the Lazy Daze, where he showered in record time. Before long, he was on his way back to Marta's house.

Evan stepped inside to escape the heat. "Hello,'' he called to warn her of his arrival.

She appeared in the doorway of her kitchen, wearing an off-white pair of casual trousers and a sleeveless green-plaid shirt. Her hair fell about her shoulders in a mass of auburn curls. "Hi.''

If wishes were horses, he'd ride over to her and carry her into the bedroom. "Are you ready to go?'' he asked.

"In a minute." She paused. "The night of Charlie's birthday party, did you mean it when you said you wanted to kiss me?"

Did a fish need water? Did the sun rise in the east? Did he dream about her every night?

"Oh, yes," he said, watching her reaction. "I still do."

Her smile was tremulous and the stiff set to her spine seemed to ease.

"Then would you?"

Her question surprised him. He hadn't expected her to be so brazen, but her white knuckles and the nervous way she licked her lips hinted at her insecurities. She'd clearly ventured out of her usual depths and he was selfish enough and eager enough to grasp his much-dreamed-about opportunity with both hands. His imagination had run rampant, and now only pure reality would satisfy him.

"You're certain?" he asked, trying to be noble and give her one last opportunity to change her mind.

"Oh, yes."

He wanted to run forward and scoop her into his arms, but he only allowed himself one step forward. "It will be hard to stop at only a kiss."

She looked startled. "Really?"

"Most definitely," he said firmly, trying to dispel all of her doubts. Had she truly not thought of herself as being desirable?

Her face turned pink. "Then what are you waiting for?"

He smiled broadly and walked closer. "I love a woman who knows her own mind."

With one long stride, he closed the distance between them. As she tipped her face to meet his, Evan wanted to grab her like a drowning man clutched a lifesaver, but he restrained himself. Instead, he lightly held her shoulders and marveled at how delicate her bones seemed in his hands.

He lowered his head, brushing his lips against hers in the briefest of contacts. Then, like magnet to metal, he pressed his mouth on hers and savored the taste.

"You smell really nice," he muttered as a part of his brain tried to identify the fragrance.

"Cucumber melon," Marta answered breathlessly. "It's—"

His mouth ended her speech. Gently, he traced a line from her temple down to her chin, moving on to stroke her bare arms before he tugged her hips against his.

She was so soft, so warm, so...*feminine*.

He moved his hand to the back of her neck and felt her silky hair lightly brush against his skin. From there, he caressed her throat before slowly descending to fiddle with the buttons of her shirt.

His fingers went lower, until he could touch the firm flesh rising above what felt like only a wisp of a bra. Her heart pounded under his palm and he ran his lips where his fingers had already traveled. Suddenly she shivered and her slight weight settled more fully against him.

Anticipation hummed through Evan's veins and the same exhilaration he experienced when he coasted down a steep slope on his bike began to build to a fever pitch. All he could think of was going the distance, flying over the edge and defying gravity to touch the sun.

"Ros...Ros is...expecting us." Marta sighed as he pushed aside the scrap of fabric and feasted on her generous curves like a starving man. He *was* starving...for her.

"She'll have to wait." He continued his gentle exploration before moving on to new and untouched territory.

"No...really. She'll call." She licked her lips and arched her back in response. "She...we...have patients waiting."

Suddenly Evan froze, uncomfortably aware of the state he'd worked himself into—how near he'd approached the point of no return. She wiggled in his arms. "Don't move."

Marta opened her eyes, blinking as if slowly coming out of a dream. "Are you OK?"

Evan gritted his teeth. "I will be in a minute." He took several long breaths, fighting for control.

"Do you want me to—?"

"Stay right there," he said, willing the pressure to ease before he disgraced himself. Reluctantly, he tucked her back in her bra and pulled the edges of her shirt closed.

"I'm sorry," she said, fastening the buttons.

He chuckled. "What for?"

"I didn't realize you would... I expected a simple kiss. Not something this..." Her voice faded.

He raised an eyebrow. "Powerful?"

A flush started at her neck and headed upwards. "Yeah."

He held her in a loose embrace. ''I had a feeling it would be this way.''

''You did?''

Evan nodded. ''Do you think Ros will send out the cavalry if we don't show up at the clinic this afternoon?''

''Not if we call and explain,'' she said pertly. ''Are you willing to spell it out for her?''

He grinned. ''I could, but since New Hope is a small town, making afternoon delight probably wouldn't be too good for your staid medical image.''

A coy smile inched its way across her face. ''No, but I could be bribed into holding special office hours this evening.''

He remembered how she'd accused him of bribing her with a kiss, and he laughed. ''If you don't mind, I'd rather make a house call.''

She moved away and struck a pose. ''Maybe I can't afford the fee.''

He grabbed her close. ''A kiss is all I need.''

CHAPTER NINE

CHICO'S funeral cast a pall over the July fourth Independence Day weekend. Although the community held its planned festivities, including a performance by the city band and the usual fireworks display, the mood didn't soar quite as high as in years past. Marta mourned with everyone else and was grateful for Evan's steady presence by her side.

It only drove home how much she would miss him when he left. He had worked too hard to reach his particular rung on the ladder of success to turn his back on everything he'd earned, but during her weaker moments she wished that he would.

Not only would she feel his absence, like any woman who missed the man she loved, but she'd miss him for professional reasons. He wouldn't be available to discuss a troubling case or to immediately deal with those situations beyond her abilities. Having a physician on site these past few weeks had been a treat for her and her patients, and she reminded herself often of how short-lived this luxury was.

For now, though, she intended to absorb as much medical knowledge as she could while Evan was here. Her next case became such a learning experience.

"Tell me how you're feeling," Marta asked the fifty-year-old farmer, who was known in the area as

Smitty rather than Clarence Smith, and who was accompanied by his wife, Claire.

"I've lost my appetite, have chills and fever and my bones ache," Smitty reported.

"Anything else?" she asked as she jotted down his comments.

"Headache. Sore throat. Stiff neck. I have trouble sleeping at night, too."

"He paces all night long," Claire supplied. A wiry woman, her skin was tanned and her blonde hair appeared bleached from the sun. "Seems he can't sit still for more than a minute. You'd think he had ants in his pants."

"Oh, Claire," Smitty grumbled. "It's not that bad. Don't be making me out to be worse than I am."

Claire glared at him, but didn't stop talking. "And irritable? My, he's like a bear who woke up too soon."

"Hush, woman," Smitty declared. "I can speak for myself." He broke into a paroxysm of coughing.

Claire waved her hand. "Then go ahead."

Smitty's jaw took on a mulish set. "I will." He glanced at Marta. "I do seem to be a little short on patience these days."

"That happens to all of us," Marta soothed. "How long have you been feeling this way?"

He thought for a minute. "About a week."

"Make that going on two," Claire corrected. "I wanted you to come in last week, remember?" She addressed Marta. "It started out mild. We thought he just had a touch of the summer flu. But then he developed this cough that won't go away."

Unfortunately, a multitude of diseases, ranging from a particularly virulent strain of influenza to something along the lines of meningitis, could account for the non-specific symptoms he'd described. Because Smitty was a normally healthy male, she refused to let a stone go unturned in her examination.

She began checking him over, carefully peering down his throat and palpating the lymph glands in his neck before listening to the rattle in his chest. She didn't need an X-ray to know this man had a case of pneumonia which would require antibiotics. However, swollen lymph glands, sore throats, headaches and restlessness didn't usually fit the picture. Something else was going on inside his body.

"Have you noticed anything else? A rash, petechiae—little red dots on your skin?" she explained.

Smitty glanced at his wife and she shrugged.

"OK. No rash. Have you done anything unusual during this time?" Marta asked. "Gone on any trips?"

"Trips? We've been too busy with harvest to even think about takin' a trip. As far as doing anything unusual, I can't think what it would be."

"Have you been exposed to any pesticides or poisons?"

"Not lately."

Claire suddenly snapped her fingers. "You were cleaning out the dead brush in our shelter belt a few weeks ago."

He sent his wife an exasperated frown. "What has cutting trees and hauling off dead limbs got to do with pesticides? I worked out there long before I got sick."

Marta began to wonder... "How long?" she asked.

Smitty drew his bushy eyebrows together as he pondered her question. "Probably close to two weeks."

An idea began to form. Although she'd decided to order a blood count and a liver-function panel, other lab tests were needed for a proper diagnosis. A spinal tap came to mind, but even if she had the supplies the procedure went beyond her scope of practice. Luckily, Evan was on hand to act as a resource.

"Do you remember being bitten by anything? Like a tick?"

He shrugged. "I don't remember, but it's possible."

"I'm going to call in Dr Gallagher," she said, scribbling more notes on her clipboard. "Or, if you prefer, I'll send you on to Dr Campbell. Dr Gallagher is an excellent physician so you needn't worry about being in good hands."

"I heard about him," Smitty said. "Bring him in. I'm all for saving me a drive to Liberal considerin' the price of gasoline these days."

She found Evan talking on the telephone and waited impatiently for him to notice her. As soon as he finished his call, she briefed him in the hallway.

"Could he have a rickettsial disease?" she asked. "He's worked in a wooded area, clearing out dead brush, and the onset of his symptoms seems to fit the incubation period."

"It's possible," Evan said. "The pneumonia could be a complication rather than the original infection. Are we able to do a spinal tap?"

"I've never kept the supplies on hand," Marta said, wishing otherwise. "I thought if the situation required an LP, the patient should be in the emergency room anyway."

"Logical, but you might consider keeping the supplies on hand. The next doctor may run into a situation where he'd want to do the tap right away."

While she made a mental note to request a few sterile packs, Evan introduced himself to Smitty and his wife. After completing his exam and reviewing Marta's notes, he sat on the small stool next to the table and addressed the couple.

"I want to admit you to the hospital," he said. "It's possible Smitty has contracted Rocky Mountain spotted fever."

"Rocky Mountain spotted fever?" Smitty echoed. "Isn't that caused by ticks up in the mountains?"

Evan smiled. "Ticks carry the disease, but you can find infected ticks anywhere there are a lot of trees. The condition is treatable, but your pneumonia concerns me. You need to be monitored closely for a few days."

"I don't need a hospital," Smitty roared. "Give me a bottle of pills and I'll go home and rest."

"I wouldn't advise that," Evan said. "You're putting yourself at risk for worse complications. Spleen and liver enlargement, an infection of the heart muscle and a host of other things can occur if you don't receive proper care."

"Smitty," Claire warned. "You gotta go."

"There's too much to do at home," he complained.

"Oh, pish!" Claire exclaimed. "There's always work waiting for us on the farm."

Marta felt compelled to add her opinion. "The neighbors will help Claire with whatever needs to be done. Remember when Felix had his kidney stone? And when Humberto broke his leg? Those are just a few of the people you've helped. Now it's your turn."

"I hate to be a bother," he mumbled.

"It's not a bother," Marta declared.

Smitty heaved a deep sigh and Marta knew they'd won the battle. "Oh, all right. But only for a few days."

Evan rose. "I'll make the arrangements while Marta draws blood." He pulled her aside. "Get a CBC, a chem panel, liver enzymes, a mono test and a blood culture times two. Collect a urine specimen, too. When does the courier arrive?"

He was referring to the lab employee who came once a day to pick up any specimens their clinic might have collected. "They'll be here in about an hour."

"Then they'll be able to start testing before Smitty arrives. I'll tell Campbell." He left to make his phone call.

Marta assembled her supplies while Smitty lay back on the table. "I'm going to poke you twice," she apologized. "Once in each arm. I promise to make it as painless as possible."

"Says the woman who's on the other side of the needle," Smitty remarked.

Marta laughed as she cleaned his left arm with a Betadine scrub. "Surely a big fellow like you isn't afraid of needles."

"Not afraid of 'em," he said. "I just don't like 'em."

Marta talked about the recent wheat harvest while she drew the required blood samples. By the time she'd finished, Evan had returned.

"Have you ever had a lumbar puncture or a spinal tap before?" he asked Smitty.

"Nope. Doesn't sound like I want to either."

Evan smiled. "It's not quite as bad as it sounds. We insert a needle into your spinal column between the vertebrae and withdraw some of the fluid. The results of the lab tests can give us a better picture of what is or isn't wrong with you."

Smitty's weather-beaten face lightened a shade or two underneath his tan and he appeared a little green around the gills. "Don't suppose you could do without this test."

"We can," Evan admitted, "but then we may misdiagnose you and prescribe the wrong antibiotic. Then you'll end up in worse shape than before."

"All right," Smitty mumbled before he coughed.

"I've notified Dr Campbell and he'll alert the hospital that you're coming. Check in at the front desk and a nurse will take you directly to a room."

Both Smitty and Claire nodded.

"Once you're there, Dr Campbell will take over."

Smitty winced. "This puncture… It sounds so… barbaric."

"It's an invasive procedure," Evan admitted. "But there are worse ones."

"Will they put me under?" he asked.

"Dr Campbell will inject a local anesthetic in the

area. You won't feel any pain, only some pressure. The worst thing will be probably be the headache afterwards, but they'll give you acetaminophen or something similar. If you have questions, just ask. Dr Campbell will explain all this again anyway.''

''Can't you just do this spinal thing here?'' Smitty asked.

''We could,'' Marta said, ''But we don't have the supplies. Even if we did we wouldn't, because it's best to monitor your blood pressure and pulse for several hours afterwards as a precaution.''

Evan ambled toward the door. ''Remember, go straight to the hospital. Dr Campbell is expecting you.''

Smitty slid off the end of the table until he'd planted his feet firmly on the floor. ''Come on, Claire. The sooner we get there, the sooner I can come home.''

The couple left, with Smitty reciting a long list of instructions. ''You'd better write this all down,'' Marta heard him say. ''You'll forget.''

''I won't forget,'' Claire declared. ''I'm sure you'll remind me fifty more times.''

Marta exchanged an amused smile with Evan as she prepared the specimens for the courier and completed the proper request forms. ''They're quite a pair.''

Evan agreed. ''I hope he won't change his mind about staying in the hospital.''

''Claire won't let him. She may seem meek and mild, but underneath she's tough.'' She sighed. ''I wish we could have done more for him here. It would have saved so much time if we could have sent the specimens on ahead.''

"Now you know and you'll prepare for the next case. In fact, why don't you see if you can enter a training program so you can collect the CSF yourself?''

"It's a good idea," she said, "but I wouldn't do them often enough to stay proficient. I'd rather stick to treating cases I encounter on a regular basis.''

"Like what?''

"Orthopedic work," she answered promptly, thinking of the three boys who'd each broken an arm while skateboarding. "To set simple fractures. I didn't apply for a preceptorship several years ago because it seemed more of a priority to get the clinic open for business.''

"Then find a temporary replacement.''

"You make it sound so easy.''

He grinned. "It is. The details are the problem.''

"No kidding.''

"Speaking of details, do you have time for a cup of coffee?'' he asked.

"Sure. Give me ten minutes or so while I write up some notes.''

Fifteen minutes later as they sat in Marta's office with their coffee Evan said, "There's something I need to—''

The buzzer in the hallway interrupted him. Before the sound died away, Ros zoomed toward them as if she were riding a gust of wind. "Claire Smith just called. Smitty is having seizures.''

"Where is she?'' Evan asked.

"At home."

"Did she call the ambulance?" Marta asked.

"I did, just now. Claire's asking for you to drive out to their place."

Marta didn't hesitate. "I'll bet you never thought you'd go on this many house calls," she said.

"No, I didn't. I don't mind, though. It beats attending parties and asking for donations."

"Yeah, that sounds like a rough life," she teased.

The couple lived two miles out of town on a country road. Luckily, Marta had raised the top on her Wrangler the night before, so they didn't have to eat dust or swelter in the July heat. She heard the ambulance's siren before she saw it a short distance ahead with its lights on. As she pulled to a stop in front of the Smith home, Walter was unloading his kit from the rear of the vehicle.

Claire called to them through the screen door of their house. They found Smitty on the floor near the entrance.

"He wanted to bring his clothes and such, so we ran home to pack a bag," she explained. "It wouldn't have taken more than a few minutes."

"It's OK," Evan assured her. "Did he drive home?"

"Yes."

"Then it was a good thing you took the detour," Evan said. "Otherwise you probably would have had an accident on the way to the hospital."

Her eyes grew wide and her voice trembled. "I hadn't thought of that."

"Tell us what happened," Evan urged.

She cleared her throat. "As soon as we came inside, he just collapsed. He was shaking, his eyes were rolled up in his head and he wouldn't respond to me."

Marta knelt next to Smitty and started an IV while Walter slipped the blood pressure cuff around his arm. Although he was no longer in the throes of his tonic-clonal seizure, there were no guarantees it wouldn't occur again.

Evan checked his pupils, nodding his agreement with Walter's silent decision to administer oxygen. "Give him diazepam IM as soon as you get the fluids running."

Marta taped down the needle in Smitty's forearm and rummaged through Walter's medical kit. She withdrew the dose Evan had indicated and injected the tranquilizer as directed.

"What happen?" Smitty's voice sounded slurred.

"You had a seizure," Evan leaned over him to say. "We've given you something to make you relax before we take you to the hospital." He muttered to Marta, "Too bad we don't have that LP kit after all."

"In...ambulance?"

"Afraid so," Evan told him, patting his shoulder. "You get to ride in style."

Walter's partner brought in the stretcher, and between the four of them they soon had Smitty strapped to the gurney with the oxygen tank lying between his legs.

Marta helped the men load their patient into the back of the ambulance. "I'll drive if you want to monitor him," Walter suggested. "Henry can bring your Jeep to the hospital so you two have a way home.''

With the travel arrangements made, their motley caravan set out, arriving in seventeen minutes instead of the usual thirty.

Conditions were cozy in the back of the ambulance but, given the choice, Marta wouldn't have been anywhere else. Although Smitty remained stable during their ride, Evan's face had settled into grim lines. She wondered if he was more concerned about their patient than he let on.

Evan spoke to Walter through the small window separating them. ''Radio ahead and ask someone to notify Dr Campbell of our ETA.''

''Gotcha.''

Two nurses met them at the ambulance bay and whisked Smitty into the nearest trauma room, where Joe Campbell was waiting.

Evan updated his colleague, and before the ink had dried on Smitty's admission papers, the two doctors were in the midst of performing his lumbar puncture.

Feeling extraneous with the two ER nurses, the two doctors and a host of other support personnel who'd appeared on the run, Marta waited in the nurses' station.

When the two men finally surfaced, they went immediately to a room and closed the door. Puzzled by their need for privacy, Marta resigned herself for another wait. Thirty minutes went by before Evan joined her.

She rose. ''How is Smitty?''

''He's resting,'' Evan said. ''We think the pneumonia and the seizures are a result of the rickettsial infection, but the lab results aren't available yet. Joe agrees with our theory, so he started him on chloramphenicol. He's also requesting serology tests to see if Smitty's been exposed to the disease.''

"I'm glad." She glanced around. "Where *is* Joe?''

"He's talking to Claire. Smitty will be in Intensive Care for a few days."

"So much for his plan to go home soon."

The double doors swung open and Joe strode through, smiling as he saw them. "Congratulations," Joe called out in his loud voice. "Evan just told me the good news. But don't worry. If everything comes to pass, we'll definitely expand the clinic's services."

He turned to Evan. "I'll keep you informed about Mr Smith."

"Thanks."

Marta was brimming with curiosity, but she held her questions until they'd reached the parking lot.

"What good news?" she asked breathlessly. "What changes? Why will I need more help?"

He stopped in his tracks. "I didn't want you to find out this way."

Staring into his face, Marta shielded her eyes from the afternoon sun. "Find out *what* this way?"

His gaze didn't waver. "A new business is moving to New Hope. It's a manufacturing facility. A test operation. If it goes well, they'll expand."

"That's wonderful!" she exclaimed, thinking of the jobs it would create. "What are they making?"

"I understand they're compressing wheat stubble

into a fiberboard material that can be used in construction.''

"Wow! This will really help New Hope,'' she said, growing excited by the prospect of the small community doubling in size. "No wonder Joe said he'd expand our services. We may be able to have our own resident physician."

"More than likely."

To her surprise, he seemed pensive. "You don't seem too happy about it," she observed.

"Why wouldn't I be? I'm all in favor of economic development, especially for New Hope."

"Then you should be jumping up and down like I am," she exclaimed, filled with too many burning questions to restrain them. "When is this industry coming? Who owns it? What made the owner choose New Hope?"

"It will be at least a year until it's fully operational. As for the owner…that's what I wanted to tell you about this afternoon." He paused. "The company belongs to your grandfather."

CHAPTER TEN

A COLD shiver slithered down Marta's spine. "My grandfather owns this company?"

Evan's gaze remained fixed on her. "Yes."

Now she understood his reticence. "When were you going to tell me?"

"This afternoon. Before I could, we went on the ambulance run with Smitty. It didn't seem appropriate to mention it while we were busy with him."

She began walking slowly to her Wrangler, pondering all the implications of Winston's latest move. Once she recovered from the shock, anger sprouted and bloomed as fast as a dandelion after a spring rain.

Her steps lengthened until she reached her vehicle. With her teeth clenched together in tight-lipped fury, she reached to unlocked the doors, but Evan grabbed the keys out of her hand.

"What are you doing?" she demanded. How dared he?

"You're upset."

"There's a news flash," she said, using her most sarcastic tone.

"You shouldn't be driving."

"I'm fine."

"Yeah, well, I'd rather make it home in one piece."

"Then rent a car."

He raised the key ring and jiggled it. "I have wheels. You don't."

"Oh, for the love of Pete," she grumbled.

"I'll drive," he said, "because if you wrap yourself around a utility pole, I don't want your accident on my conscience."

In answer, she glared at him. He raised an eyebrow and for a moment a silent battle of wills raged.

"Please, Marta," he said, his tone softer…kinder. "Get in. I'll take us home."

Pursing her lips, she stomped to the passenger side and crawled in. After fastening her seat belt, she crossed her arms and stared through the side window.

Evan slowly reversed out of the stall, then navigated through the city streets toward the highway. She stewed in silence until they were halfway to New Hope.

"Say something," he demanded.

"Were you in on this?"

"You mean, did I know he was going to start an industry in New Hope?" She nodded and he continued, "No. I heard the news for the first time this morning."

Marta brushed the loose tendrils of hair away from her face. "What's he trying to prove?"

"As far as I know, nothing."

"Nothing?" She scoffed. "Winston doesn't do anything without an ulterior motive."

She could see the headlines, hear everyone in town singing his praises. Once people knew of her ties to Winston, her life would turn upside down. Public opinion would sway to his side, and she'd be classed as the ungrateful wretch who had turned her back on her grandfather. What a well-calculated move on his part.

"I won't be manipulated," she declared.

Evan gripped the steering-wheel and his jaw tightened as if he were trying to hold onto his temper. "Why can't you accept he just wants to do something nice for your town?"

"Because he's never done anything nice for anyone before. I've read his interviews. Cut-throat, ruthless, single-minded, a barracuda. Those are all the adjectives people have used to describe him."

"He wouldn't be so successful if he was a doormat. The business world isn't for the faint-hearted. Besides, you can't believe everything you read."

"Must you always defend him?" she demanded.

"Must you always find fault?" he countered. "The man wants to do something for you. For *you*, Marta. And because you won't allow him the opportunity, he's willing to do something for the entire town.

"This is the old the-water-glass-is-half-full-or-half-empty routine. Sure, you can either vilify what he's doing or recognize it as a generous act. The choice is yours."

Marta fell silent, vaguely noting they'd reached the New Hope city limits. "I'd like to believe he's as altruistic as you claim, but…" She shook her head. She simply couldn't stretch her imagination that far.

"You are, without a doubt, the most stubborn woman I've ever run across."

"Speak for yourself," she returned. "Why won't you understand my side of the story?"

"Because I *don't* understand. Let go of your teen-age anger. Yes, I feel bad for you about that day, but I can't change what happened no matter how much I might want to.

"You're not the same person you were thirteen years ago," Evan continued. "Neither is Winston. Judge him by today's actions, not yesterday's. And judge him for yourself, not by what the media says."

He paused. "You give everyone else three strikes—why won't you give him the same courtesy?"

A long moment passed and her anger built. "It's easy for you to say forget the past and give him another chance, but you're not risking anything."

Evan pulled into the clinic's parking lot and slammed on the brakes before he shoved the gearshift into neutral and switched off the ignition.

"I'm risking a helluva lot," he ground out, his eyes spitting fire.

"Like what?"

"My future. *Our* future."

Nothing else he could have said would have deflated her anger as fast. "Our future?" Marta repeated.

"Our future," he stated firmly. "As much as I want you in my life until we're both gumming our food and holding wheelchair races, Winston is already there. I'm willing to compromise on a lot of things— hell, I'll even spend my summers in New Hope if that's what you want—but Winston is as much a member of my family as my mother."

Tears blurred her vision. As a declaration of love,

it lacked something, but knowing how he felt simply added to her inner turmoil.

He let out a sharp, heartfelt sigh. "I'd stay and talk some sense into you, but I have to drive back to Dallas. I suspect I'd be wasting my breath anyway."

She focused on a few of his words. "You're leaving?"

"There's a major problem at the hospital with the government Medicare inspectors. The CEO wants all the department staff available tomorrow to answer questions. I need to be in my office bright and early."

Fate had robbed her of what had been shaping up to be the best summer in twenty-eight years. "Will you...?" She cleared the lump in her throat. "Will you finish your vacation when the crisis is over?"

What she really wanted to know was if he would return to New Hope. She waited on tenterhooks for his answer.

His smile seemed forced. "No. It's time I went back to work. Part of the reason for this vacation was to re-evaluate my career. Working with you helped me put everything in perspective."

He was going back to his country club, dinner parties and wealthy friends. So much for her dream of him wanting to practice in New Hope. "I thought you didn't like the fund-raising scene."

"I don't, but if convincing a few people to donate money will help kids like Charlie, then I'm willing to do it."

"Will I see you again?" She hated the weepy note in her voice.

He hesitated. "It's up to you," he finally said. "I

want you at my side, but it's an all-or-nothing prop-
osition. I don't want to feel guilty if I spend time with
Winston and I don't want you to be angry when I do.
So here's something to think about when you're alone
at night…''

He reached across the console and pulled her into
his arms. Her mouth eagerly met his in a kiss capable
of igniting wet tinder. She clung to him, trying to etch
every sensation she felt on her mind.

He broke away with what sounded like a groan. In
the next instant, he was gone.

Pain like she'd never known before filled her chest
and made it almost impossible to breathe. She stum-
bled into the clinic, hardly able to see because of the
tears brimming in her eyes.

She staggered to her office where she sank behind
the desk. Evan's scent hung in the air as a bitter-sweet
reminder of the past few weeks.

Ros's wheels whispered against the linoleum.
''What's wrong? And where's Dr Gallagher? Oh, my
gosh. Is Smitty…?''

Marta blew her nose. ''Smitty's in ICU, but he'll
be fine,'' she said, tossing the tissue into the trash.
''Evan's gone.''

''He's gone?''

''He went back to Dallas. Some problem with the
hospital and he has to help sort things out.''

''Is he coming back?''

The lump in Marta's throat reappeared. She shook
her head.

Ros rolled forward to place her hand on Marta's.
''I'm sorry.''

Marta dug deep inside for the strength she'd called upon many times in her life. "Don't be," she said more sharply than she intended. "He has his career and I have mine. It was better for both of us if he left before…before our emotions got in the way."

Actually, it was too late. Her emotions were already involved. She'd fallen in love for the first time in her life.

"Clean breaks are always for the best," Ros said.

"Absolutely." But why did they have to hurt so much?

"Have you heard anything about Jim Carter?" Ros asked Marta a week later.

"Dr Tubman diagnosed testicular cancer, just like Evan suspected," Marta said, hoping she didn't sound as if she was pining after the man. Although she'd smiled and joked and acted as usual, inside she felt empty.

"Too bad. Is he going to be OK?"

"He'll have chemo, but he was in the early stages. I'll bet he's glad that steer ran into him, otherwise he might not have noticed the lump until it was too late."

"No kidding." Ros wheeled herself closer to the window in her office. "Guess who just pulled in?"

Let it be Evan, Marta thought, crossing her fingers and forcing herself not to run to the window and look for herself. Yet she knew it wouldn't be him. She didn't need Ros's handwriting analysis to tell her that once he reached a decision he stuck to it. Besides, if a black Lexus had arrived, Ros would be jumping up and down, not moaning.

The only other person who could instill such dread in Ros was... "Don't tell me." She had her own problems—she wasn't in the mood to deal with Monica's.

"All right. I won't. You can be surprised."

"It's Monica, isn't it?"

"You said not to tell you," Ros reminded her.

"What if I sneak out the back door?"

"We don't have a back door."

"Darn." Marta watched Monica walk through their entrance. To her surprise, Monica's shoulders were straight and she wore a tan skirt and a leopard-print blouse to match.

"Hello," she said cheerfully.

"You look nice today," Ros commented.

Monica blushed a pretty pink. "Why, thank you. I wondered if I could have a few words with Dr Gallagher."

"He's not here any more," Marta explained. "He only worked here temporarily."

Monica's smile turned down. "I'm sorry to hear it. I wanted to tell him how much I appreciated his advice."

"Did you see a counselor?"

"No, I went to my minister. He's a widower, you know," she said, patting her hair in place. "Anyway, to make a long story short, he helped me to see how I was suppressing my anger toward my children and it was making me sick."

"I'm glad you're better," Marta said.

Monica smiled. "Thanks to Dr Gallagher, I don't plan on dropping in to see you nearly as often. Will you let him know?"

"The next time I talk to him," Marta promised, although she didn't know when, or if, she ever would.

"Bye, now."

Once Marta and Ros were alone, Ros burst out laughing. "If you could have seen the look on your face."

"On my face? What about yours?"

"Sounds as if Evan saved the day for her."

This constant talk of Evan sent a familiar pain through Marta's stomach. "Yeah. Have you seen my bottle of antacids?"

"Nope. Don't tell me you're out again."

"I've just misplaced them," she said defensively. "That's all. Don't make a big deal out of it."

"Out of curiosity, when *are* you going to talk to Evan?"

Marta avoided Ros's gaze. "I don't know." She'd watched CNN nightly for the latest in the government's investigation of St Margaret's, eager to catch a glimpse of Evan during their reports. Unfortunately, she never did. Now that the inspectors had issued a press release, stating they'd found no evidence of fraud, CNN would move on to other stories and she could stop thinking about Evan Gallagher.

"Maybe you should call."

If Ros only knew how many times she'd picked up the phone, then stopped herself. Until she was willing to accept Winston as a valued part of Evan's family, she was wasting her time.

"He's made his decision..." She remembered his challenge to her and his subsequent kiss. Her memory of those few seconds still had the power to wake her from a sound sleep with his name on her lips.

"You're being stubborn again."

"If he really loved me, he shouldn't have any trouble choosing between Winston and me."

"If *you* really loved *him*," Ros countered, "you wouldn't put him in the position of having to choose in the first place."

She'd never thought of it in that way. Ignoring the painful jab of truth, she argued, "They're both trying to manipulate me."

"Where did you get this idea?"

"My mother told me how her father was always forcing her to do things she didn't want to do. She had to attend the school he chose, not the one she wanted. She had to associate with the friends he'd deemed acceptable, not the ones she chose. He even selected the man he wanted her to marry. It's no wonder she rebelled." The idea of making peace with Winston Clay had always seemed like a betrayal of her mother's memory.

"I'm not trying to undermine your mom, but have you stopped to consider how we, especially as teenagers, have a skewed image of the world? We see what we want to see."

"If you're implying—"

Ros held up her hands. "I'm not implying anything. I'm simply saying there are two sides to everything. Maybe your grandfather *was* a tyrant and ran his home like a prison. On the other hand, maybe he was over-protective and didn't want to risk losing his only child. It's not unheard of for someone to kidnap a child of a wealthy family and hold them for ransom. If my net worth came anywhere close to his, I'd place a lot of restrictions on my kids, too."

"You're watching too many movies," Marta scoffed, although another seed of doubt had been planted.

"Hey, I'm just speculating. As I said, every coin has two sides. Just remember, pride and unforgiveness are mighty cold bedfellows. Ask Monica Taylor how happy she was before she let go of the past."

Marta slumped into a chair. She was tired. Tired of her thoughts racing around like a hamster on an exercise wheel.

Ros wheeled herself close to Marta. "Now, be honest. How much do you miss him?"

"Terribly," she admitted.

"I know you don't believe in my little hobby, but you have to admit how all the characteristics you saw in him firsthand also surfaced in his handwriting. Honesty, loyalty, determination, confidence. I can't believe you're letting him slip through your fingers."

She didn't want to. She wanted to hang on tight. But the skeleton in her closet was terribly scary.

"And stop trying to punish your grandfather," Ros declared.

It was an interesting concept… "Is that what I'm doing?" Marta wondered aloud.

"I think so."

If refusing to see her grandfather was the punishment she was trying to inflict on him, then, if she continued to do so, she would lose out on something near and dear to her.

Ros shrugged. "Of course, if holding your grudge against your grandfather is more important than having Evan around, then I say hang onto it. Who needs a husband anyway?"

Marta closed her eyes and pictured Evan's smiling face.

Judge him for yourself. Give him a second chance like you give everyone else.

Instantly, she knew what she had to do. She wanted...no, *deserved*...a future, and no one, especially Winston Clay, would take it from her.

She sat up straight. "Cancel all my appointments tomorrow."

Ros raised one eyebrow. "Why?"

"I'm going out of town."

Ros crossed her arms and smiled broadly. "The girl has finally come to her senses. Are you sure you'll only need one day? Dallas isn't in our back yard, you know."

Marta smiled. "I'll let you know."

Marta strode into the lobby of the Clay Enterprises Building the next afternoon, wearing the expensive new hunter green sheath she'd just purchased. She'd thought that if she spent what seemed like a million dollars, she'd feel that way, too.

So far it wasn't working. In fact, she was wondering if she'd lost all good sense by putting herself through this agony.

Her palms were sweaty and each step seemed as if

she were trying to walk out of quicksand. She punched the 'up' elevator button and stepped inside.

The attendant, in her pristine, military-style uniform, asked, "What floor, please?"

Marta cleared her throat. "Ten."

The woman pressed the button and the elevator whizzed upwards, leaving Marta's stomach in her black pumps. In a twinkling of an eye, she reached her destination and the doors slid apart. "Your floor, miss," she said.

Marta drew a deep breath, gave her a tremulous smile and stepped into the hallway. Everything was the same, yet different. The decor was more modern, the color scheme more current, but she still remembered the basic floor plan.

Winston Clay's gold name-plate hadn't changed, but she had. She wasn't a meek teenager any more. She was a person who'd made her way in the world through her own blood, sweat and tears.

Wiping her palms on her dress, she squared her shoulders and opened the door.

The desk stood in the same spot, although Ms Lancaster wasn't the woman sitting at it. This secretary was in her mid-fifties and looked as if she ate choke-cherries for lunch. She peered at a computer screen and typed at a speed Ros would have envied.

"I'd like to see Mr Clay," Marta announced.

"Do you have an appointment?" she asked.

"No."

"He's in conference right now and can't be disturbed."

The perfect test had fallen in her lap. "Tell him that Marta Wyman is here."

"I'm afraid it's impossible. He's in the middle of international negotiations."

Resolve welled up inside her. She leaned both hands on the desk and leaned close to the secretary. "Either you tell him or I'll walk in there myself."

"This is highly irregular."

Marta smiled, ready to do battle. She'd come this far and *no one* would turn her from her course. "I'm a nurse," she mentioned offhandedly. "If regularity is a problem, I suggest you add more fiber to your diet."

The woman gasped. Frowning, she jumped to her feet and scrambled toward the set of double doors behind her desk. Peering at Marta over her shoulder and giving her another glare for good measure, she opened the right-hand door just enough to slip through.

Too nervous to sit in the plush chairs, Marta paced the floor and studied the magazines on the coffee-table. News, sports and business periodicals lay in an artful array, all current issues and all without a single crease of the pages. Quite a difference from the dog-eared copies in her waiting room.

Suddenly both doors swung wide and banged against the wall. Marta turned, and her heart seemed to stop.

The man she remembered, the tall man with the graying hair, harsh expression and cold eyes, stood framed in the opening. She swallowed hard as the urge to flee came over her. Her feet, however, wouldn't move, and she remained glued to the floor.

Winston Clay's serious demeanor slowly softened as he searched her face. In another instant a full smile spread from ear to ear and he took one step forward.

"Marta!" he cried, his joy unmistakable. "You came!"

His secretary interrupted. "Mr Clay. What shall I do about your conference call?"

"Explain to the gentlemen that we'll finish our discussion later."

"They'll want to know the reason for the delay."

Winston's gaze never left Marta's. "Nothing is more important than family, Mrs Erickson. Tell them I've found my lost sheep. My granddaughter has come home."

One word, "granddaughter", broke through the brick walls surrounding Marta's heart, and the fear in her heart crumbled into dust. Tears welled in her eyes and, without warning, they streamed down her face faster than she could brush them away.

As he opened his arms to welcome her, she didn't hesitate. She walked, then ran into the comfort of his embrace. She truly had come home.

Evan strode into Winston's mansion through the entrance designated for deliveries. It led toward the kitchen where he usually found his mother, and today wasn't an exception.

He kissed her cheek. "Hi, Mom. What's cooking?"

"Your favorite. Caesar salad, beef tips with rice,

steamed vegetables and double chocolate cake for dessert.''

''What's the occasion?''

Ruth stirred the contents of a pan on the stove. ''Why do you ask?''

''Sounds sort of fancy for a middle-of-the-week meal.''

She shrugged. ''I cook what Winston requests. I imagine he wants to celebrate how well things turned out at the hospital.''

''Could be.'' He grabbed a cheese-stuffed celery stick and chomped down. ''Where is he?''

''In his den.''

''OK.'' He headed through the saloon doors toward Winston's office, wishing the evening was ending rather than just beginning. The older man was trying to cheer him up by inviting him to dinner, but he wasn't in the mood for idle chit-chat even if it took place over a wonderful meal.

Losing Jill to her ex-husband had hurt, but losing Marta was far worse. Although the investigation at St Margaret's had occupied a great deal of his time, he'd dreamt of Marta calling. He'd asked for his phone messages so often in the hope of finding one from her that he'd offended his extremely efficient secretary.

Marta was in his thoughts constantly and it was driving him to distraction. He would walk through the hospital and hear her voice, see the same-colored hair or smell her familiar scent, but she wouldn't be there.

Right now was a prime example. He could swear Marta's perfume lingered on the air. He really must be losing his grip. Something had to be done and, by heaven, he was going to take matters into his own hands.

If he had to hogtie her and bring her to Dallas, he would, because he couldn't live like this any more. He would go to New Hope in the morning and nothing would sway him from his course. His decision was final. He absolutely, positively would persuade Marta to face the past because she wouldn't have to do it alone. He would walk beside her every step of the way.

Winston met him outside of his den. "Evan! So good of you to come on such short notice."

Evan forced a note of enthusiasm. "Dinner smells wonderful."

"Ruth has outdone herself tonight." Winston waved toward his office. "Go on in and make yourself comfortable. I'll be right back. Forgot my glasses."

Evan pointed. "They're in your pocket."

Winston patted his shirtfront. "So they are. Well, then, I must have forgotten something else. Your mother will figure it out. Now, go on in and relax." Before Evan could argue, Winston disappeared through the saloon doors.

Evan shook his head. It wasn't like the man who negotiated million-dollar deals to be so…unsettled. Perhaps he'd explain while they ate.

He opened the door and once again swore that Marta had been in the room. "Get real," he muttered under his breath.

As if his mere thought had conjured up her image, she appeared before him. "Hi, Evan," she said softly.

"Marta?" He blinked, wondering if his last cup of coffee had been spiked and he was hallucinating.

She nodded. "Yes. How are you?"

"I'm fine. Are you really here?"

She smiled. "I think so. My arms are black and blue from pinching myself, so this isn't a dream."

If it was, he didn't want to wake up. "Does Winston know you're here? Of course he does," he thought aloud.

Marta giggled. "Actually, he planned this. I went to his office this afternoon and we talked."

"You did? How was your first meeting?"

"Stressful," she admitted, "but it turned out like I'd wanted it to thirteen years ago."

"I'm glad. Did he explain things?"

"A little. We talked more about the present. And the future."

"And what kind of future did you two work out?"

"We'll see quite a bit of each other." She clenched her hands together. "He'll fly to New Hope for business and I'll drive to Dallas for fun. Unless..." Her voice faded.

Evan was curious. "Unless what?"

"Unless I'm living here."

"Do you want to live in the city?" he asked cautiously.

"It depends."

"On what?"

"On who I'm going to live with. You see, someone once asked me if I'd ever leave New Hope."

He remembered the conversation vividly. "You said you would if the right person came along."

"Yes. I found him. I'm just waiting for him to ask."

Evan strode forward and took her hands. They were like blocks of ice. "Will you move in with me? Be my wife, my friend, my partner?"

She smiled. "Until we're old enough to gum our food and hold wheelchair races with Ros."

Her quote of his words made him laugh, and he hugged her. "I can't believe this is happening. I never thought you'd change your mind. I was prepared to drive to New Hope tomorrow and drag you here by your hair." He held her at arm's length. "What *did* change your mind?"

"I love you. Fate robbed me of a lot of things. I didn't want it to steal you, too."

He tipped up her chin to stare directly into her eyes. "And I love you. We're going to have a great life together," he vowed.

"I know we will, but we also have a lot of issues to work out. I can't leave New Hope until I've found a replacement. Then I'll need to find a job—"

"We have plenty of time to sort out the details," he said, swinging her in a circle. "What do you say we fly this coop and find someplace perfect for just the two of us?"

"We can't." She sounded horrified. "Your mother and my grandfather have organized a candlelight dinner on the patio. We can't leave when they've worked so hard to arrange this for us."

"They won't mind."

"I will," she said firmly. "I haven't had the grand

tour yet but, as big as this place is, after dinner we could disappear and no one would find us.''

Evan grinned. ''That, my love, is a devious idea and one I heartily endorse. Let's eat.''

''Evan,'' she scolded lightly, ''they haven't called us, so the food isn't ready. You'll have to be patient and think of something to do in the meantime.''

''I already have the perfect activity in mind.''

Bending his head, he kissed her.

Ruth stirred the gravy once more. ''Do you think we should serve dinner now? The beef is almost as tough as shoe leather.''

Winston stood on the other side of the saloon doors and cocked his head in the direction of his office. The laughter he heard had banished the heaviness he'd carried in his heart for nearly thirty years.

''Ah, Ruth. They're young and need time alone.''

''But my entrée will be ruined,'' she wailed.

''Then we'll order pizza. They're too besotted with each other to notice the difference.''

Ruth tiptoed to the door and listened. ''It's gotten awfully quiet.''

A smile of satisfaction spread across his face. ''That, my dear woman, is the sound of love.''

MILLS & BOON®

Makes any time special™

Mills & Boon publish 29 new titles every month. Select from...

Modern Romance™   Tender Romance™

Sensual Romance™

Medical Romance™ Historical Romance™

MAT2

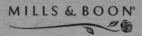

MILLS & BOON®

Medical Romance™

COMING HOME TO DANIEL *by Josie Metcalfe*

Denison Memorial Hospital

Believing that Daniel had died five years ago, Sam had comforted herself that at least she had his son to care for. But on returning home to take up a new locum position, she found Daniel alive and well—with a son only a few months older than their own!

DR MATHIESON'S DAUGHTER *by Maggie Kingsley*

Book two of St Stephen's Accident and Emergency duo

When Specialist Registrar and confirmed bachelor Dr Elliot Mathieson finds out he's a father, he begs his good friend, nurse Jane Halden for help. She can't refuse him, though maybe she should. Unknown to Elliot, Jane's been in love with him for years!

THE NURSE'S DILEMMA *by Gill Sanderson*

Book one of Nursing Sisters duo

Kate had always been a wanderer, but when she returned home, she found a reason to stay in Dr Steve Russell. However, he loved Kate because she wasn't looking for commitment and if she told him she loved him, she'd almost certainly lose him…

On sale 1st June 2001

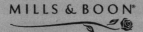

MILLS & BOON®

Medical Romance™

THE HONOURABLE DOCTOR *by Carol Wood*

Book one of Country Partners duo

Dr Marcus Granger and Dr Jane Court had been passionately in love, but she let Marcus marry her best friend, who was pregnant and terminally ill. Seven years later, widower Marcus is back. Can Jane ever forgive him for doing the honourable thing?

A HUSBAND TO TRUST *by Judy Campbell*

The day Mike Corrigan joined St Luke's as the new casualty doctor was the day that Sister Lindy Jenkins should have been married. Mike made it clear he was attracted to Lindy but if she risked her heart again, could he really be a husband to trust?

MIDWIFE UNDER FIRE! *by Fiona McArthur*

Midwife Noni Frost's maternity unit desperately needs to hire a new obstetrician, or it will be closed down. Obstetrician Iain McCloud tells her he is just a surgeon as he has reasons why he can't stay. But then he falls for Noni—how can he tell her the truth?

On sale 1st June 2001

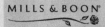

FREE!

4 Books
and a surprise gift!

We would like to take this opportunity to thank you for reading this Mills & Boon® book by offering you the chance to take FOUR more specially selected titles from the Medical Romance™ series absolutely FREE! We're also making this offer to introduce you to the benefits of the Reader Service™ —

- ★ FREE home delivery
- ★ FREE gifts and competitions
- ★ FREE monthly Newsletter
- ★ Books available before they're in the shops
- ★ Exclusive Reader Service discounts

Accepting these FREE books and gift places you under no obligation to buy; you may cancel at any time, even after receiving your free shipment. Simply complete your details below and return the entire page to the address below. **You don't even need a stamp!**

YES! Please send me 4 free Medical Romance books and a surprise gift. I understand that unless you hear from me, I will receive 6 superb new titles every month for just £2.49 each, postage and packing free. I am under no obligation to purchase any books and may cancel my subscription at any time. The free books and gift will be mine to keep in any case.

MIZEB

Ms/Mrs/Miss/Mr ....Initials...
BLOCK CAPITALS PLEASE

Surname..

Address..

....

....Postcode ....

Send this whole page to:
UK: The Reader Service, FREEPOST CN81, Croydon, CR9 3WZ
EIRE: The Reader Service, PO Box 4546, Kilcock, County Kildare (stamp required)